In *Storms of the Mind*, Pusonnam Yiri not only executes a fantastic story, packed with connections, emotions and experiences, he goes a step further by making the lessons learned within the story, lessons that are beneficial to everyone reading the book.

This book brought laughter, smiles, heartache, and a realization of the heart of which many books do not do. Lessons are learned in every page of this book, and in the end the answer is revealed. This book not only makes situations real, it also brings hope, and shows how love can transform people. Through the love of one Man, we are all saved, but there must be a seeking first and when we seek, we will find.

Most Reverend (Dr.) Nemuel Babba
Archbishop LCCN

"Storms of the Mind" is the third and most exciting of Pusonnam Yiri's true-to-life novels. Each chapter will leave you eager to know what happens next! Once again we are brought face to face with life issues and challenges familiar to us all, in marriage, family, business and society. The solutions, according to the author, are not to be found in a theory, philosophy, religion or political agenda, but in a *person*, a totally unique Person. We highly recommend this valuable book.

Dr. Robert & Mrs. Janet Dann
Bible teachers and editors,
Chester, UK.

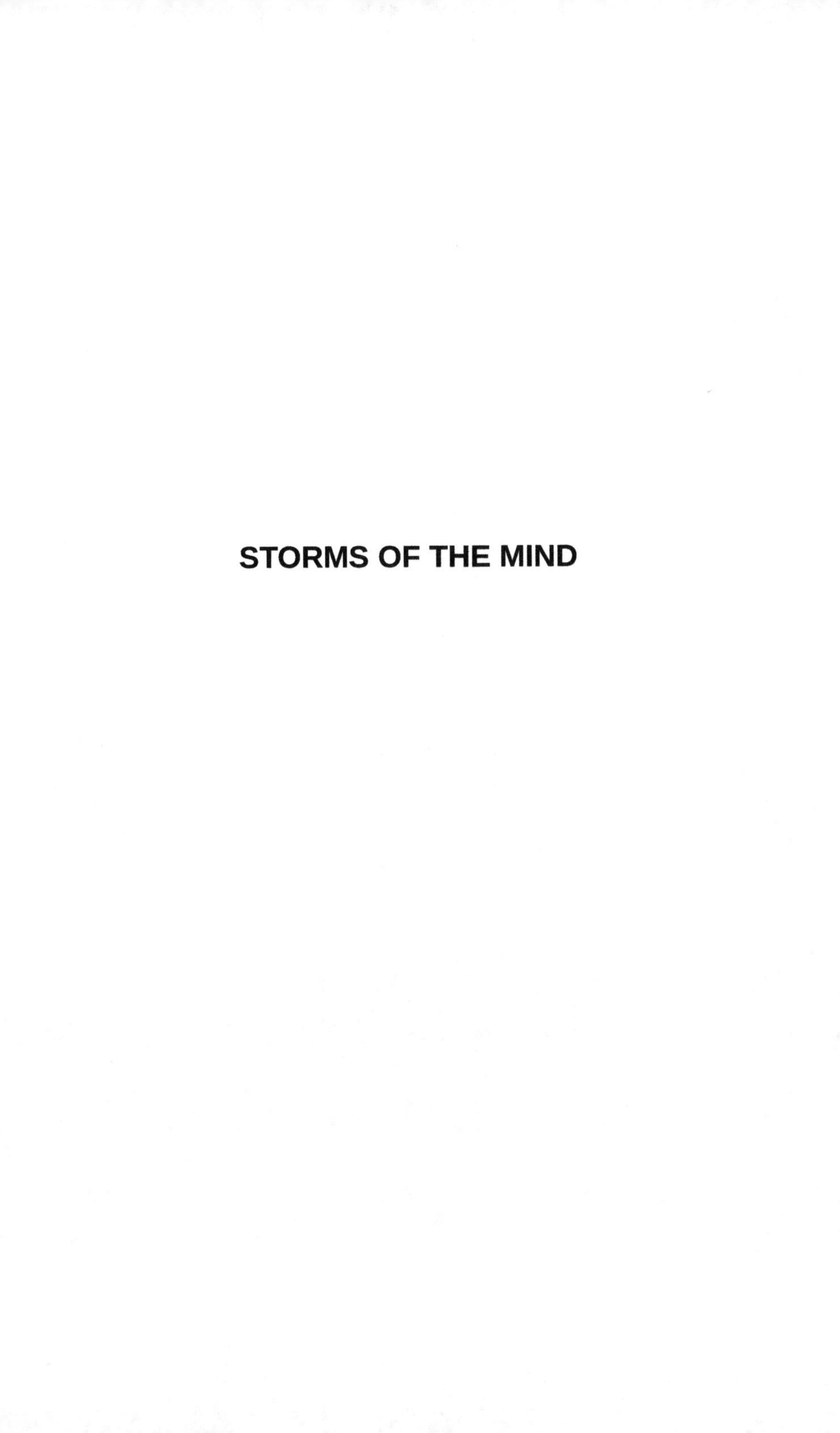

STORMS OF THE MIND

Storms of the Mind

Freedom is a Choice

Pusonnam Yiri

AFRICA CHRISTIAN TEXTBOOKS

2015

Storms of the Mind

© 2013, 2015 by Pusonnam Yiri

Africa Christian Textbooks (ACTS)

ACTS Bookshop, International HQ, TCNN,
PMB 2020, Bukuru, Plateau State, 930008, Nigeria
GSM: +234 (0) 803-589-5328; E-mail: info@acts-ng.com
Website: http://www.acts-ng.com

ISBN: 978-978-905-246-2 Print
ISBN: 978-978-905-247-9 ePub
ISBN: 978-978-905-248-6 Mobi

For further information, contact: 08105397509. Email: pusonnamyiri@gmail.com

Previously published ISBN: 978-978-935-524-2

DEDICATION

For the ministry of reconciliation

CONTENTS

ACKNOWLEDGEMENTS

My first appreciation is to God, who created me with the ability to write for His glory. Without Him, I cannot do anything.

I thank my wife, Helen, for her love and contributions in proofreading. I also thank my children for their patience and support.

Further appreciation goes to my father, late Rev. J.D. Yiri, and my mother, Mrs. Grace Yiri, who taught me the ways of the Lord from childhood.

My editors have made relevant contributions by God's grace. I really thank God for their gifts and passion in ensuring that the book is of high universal standard: Mr. Androcules Murray, Dr. and Mrs. Robert Dann, Rev. Jerry Faruk, Associate Prof. Mark Hopkins and Dr. W. Paul Todd

I thank the Archbishop of the Lutheran Church of Christ in Nigeria, Most Rev. Nemuel Babba for his encouragement.

I appreciate Dr. Sid Garland, Rev. Luka Vandi, Rev. Samuel Goro, Rev. Alen Tanko, and others, for their encouragement.

I am also grateful to Blessing Timkat, who contributed in the proof reading. I thank all members and partners of our ministry.

INTRODUCTION

Everyone can find the Answer.

Crises across the world are leading many people to frustration. Nations, organizations, individuals and families desire peace.

In addition, many people with a great deal of potential are ignored and do not have adequate opportunities to flourish. The few that do have resources often focus those on themselves, their immediate family members and friends. Many of those going through frustration have no option; but to respond according to their own rules.

Do we really have answers to all these burning issues? In STORMS OF THE MIND, the Person rejected by many is the Solution the world needs.

The tribal names in the book are from Mbula tribe in Adamawa State, Nigeria. Some of the names have not been spelt in their original Mbula spelling background, but in consideration of the context of English language.

CHAPTER 1

A wild beast was hungry and fiercely chasing Nachau. Its speed was beyond Nachau's efforts to reach the nearest village and jump into the nearby river. He was afraid and could sense death approaching. The beast ran faster and faster as it hunted Nachau, ignoring the other animals that were its usual food. Disaster struck, a few meters to the river as the beast jumped on Nachau, grabbed his throat, and pulled him down while blood gushed out from the wounds. The beast was focused on his complete destruction. In spite of the difficulty in breathing and loss of blood, Nachau, however, refused to give up. Suddenly, he felt a strange strength within him, and tightly squeezed the beast's throat until it had no option, but to retreat from its mission of devouring him.

Suddenly, Akio heard a terrible shout. "Honey, what is wrong?" she asked curiously while tapping her husband on the back.

Nachau woke up in confusion and remained silent for a moment.

"What is wrong?" Akio inquired further.

"I had another nightmare."

"Again?"

"The same nightmare as the two I had earlier," Nachau lamented.

"They must be pointing towards the same thing."

Nachau kept quiet for awhile. "I sense that our next mission will present terrible challenges, but will eventually be fruitful. That is why I have had this dream repeatedly to discourage me from preparing well."

"What assignment are you talking about?" Akio asked with concern.

"When the right time comes, everything will be clear. Let us pray."

Nachau and Akio prayed for protection and clarity for the next mission. After that, sleep came easily for Nachau; but Akio lost her desire for it.

Nachau has the gift of encouragement. He believes that everyone has a role to play in God's master plan. No one remains the same after meeting him. He is also an author who has written some books that are helpful to many people.

^

"For the sake of unity between us, I give my daughter Yalami in marriage to your son Ganduro," Amsami said, as he handed over Yalami to Ganduro. Women from the two neighbouring villages, Romen and Kiringa, responded with shouting and dancing, singing joyful songs in the family house of Amsami.

The reception ground became dusty because of the dance. That didn't discourage members of the two villages from eating, and drinking local and bottled beer. Their favourite was the bottled beer, because it was not easy for them to buy it. Now that it was available, they took full advantage of the opportunity. They also presented gifts to the bride and groom, encouraging them to continue to love each other and maintain the unity between the two villages. Drummers had a wonderful day. They beat their drums with passion as if there were no tomorrow.

Ganduro and Yalami danced with joy. Their friends also joined them in the dance. Some people were showering them with money. It was also a moment for young women and men to engage in finding new friends.

No wonder other villages admired the unity between Romen and Kiringa. Particularly in politics, the two villages were influential in different aspects of life. Their population was a major determining factor in political decisions in Naren Local Government Area.

The level of intermarriages among them was high and one of their major sources of unity. The people were mostly into farming and fishing. Most of the young men and women had not had the opportunity of 'O' level education. Some had it, but could not progress further to university level. The few schools in the villages lacked qualified teachers and basic amenities. Most parents preferred having their children helping on the farms and fishing to schooling. As a result, life was difficult for both the parents and children. It became a way of life for most of the young men and women to meet in a place they called "Mariban" for drinking local brewed beer and chatting with friends.

Calvin, one of the people working for change among the people of both villages, had tried many ideas to help the youth discover their potential and make better use of their time, but none of his efforts had received the desired response. The only Church that could help him achieve his goal in the area, headed by Pastor Namo, usually opposed him, fearing that Calvin would establish another Church denomination besides his own. This concerned Calvin. He had expected the pastor to join with him as a partner in helping people to discover and achieve the purpose of life.

Calvin's lifestyle in the past was rough. He was an armed robber, who was converted for good after meeting Nachau. Since then, he had a burden of ensuring that people, especially in rural areas, were reached with the right encouragement that could help them achieve more in life.

^

Driving in an expensive car, Lah looked as if all hope was gone. He couldn't relax despite the comfort of his car. His problems were seriously bothering him. His beard looked rough because he had not shaved for some days. He was a rich man of more than fifty years of age, who had inherited a business from his parents. As the Chief Executive Officer of the company, he had unsuccessfully tried many ways of becoming effective.

On getting to Nachau's house, he horned. The security man came out. Lah checked with the security man that he was at the right place. The security man asked him some questions before answering Lah's question to avoid giving information to the wrong person. Eventually, he opened the gate and Lah drove into the compound.

Nachau's house had a beautiful garden that served as a thinking corner for Nachau. The grass in the compound was green and fruit-bearing trees were at their best. Immediately Lah alighted from the car, the security man directed him to the door. Lah's face was still looking sad as he knocked at the door. Quickly, Mijah, Nachau's son, opened the door and greeted Lah politely. Lah replied asking Mijah for his father. Mijah asked Lah to come in and have a seat.

When Lah entered, he sat cautiously admiring the artistic decoration and neatness of the parlour. His mind was dwelling on how he wished to be more successful since he was ageing fast. That his friends, who, despite being younger than him, were more successful disturbed his mind. He wished that his managers would consider being faithful with the way they managed his resources.

Nachau walked expectantly into the parlour to see his guest. His mind was immediately curious when he saw him. His guest's mood made him realise that another huge assignment was confronting him.

"Good afternoon," Nachau greeted.

"Good afternoon, sir," Lah responded, as he stood up to shake hands with Nachau.

"Please, have a seat."

"Thank you."

Both of them sat down.

"I am Lah," he introduced himself.

"I am Nachau Turomale."

"I know. That is why I am here."

Nachau smiled. "What can I do for you?"

"I heard that you help people to discover and use their potential."

"I am able to help people only by God's grace," Nachau calmly replied.

Lah kept quiet for about a minute. Nachau also kept quiet, waiting for him to finish the journey of thoughts in his mind.

"I am more than fifty years old," Lah disclosed. "I have some resources that I believe could help the growth of many people, but my problem is that most of the people managing the resources are selfish and corrupt. As a result, I experience difficulties in using them."

"What job do you do?"

"I own an oil company."

"That means you are a rich man."

Lah smiled in acknowledgment. "My main concern is to ensure that all the people working in my company experience a better life."

Nachau listened.

"Some of the problems I face are: corruption by most of my managers, destruction of some major pipelines by some aggrieved members of our host community, religious and tribal divisions among my members of staff and lack of commitment by most of the staff towards the growth of the company."

"I am happy you have these problems and you were able to identify them," Nachau responded after silence for a moment.

"I don't understand," Lah said anxiously.

"Problems lead to creativity. New ideas wouldn't have come up without problems."

Lah nodded.

"A patient, whose disease is yet to be diagnosed, easily becomes a victim of wrong drugs in managing his case. It is only when the right diagnosis is made that the right drug can be prescribed. In a similar way, identifying the problems you face in your company is the beginning of healing."

"I get your point."

"On the issue of your workers, I commend you for having good intention towards them. I will be willing to help you improve by God's grace so that you can fully achieve your potential."

"I will be glad to listen to your ideas," Lah remarked joyfully.

"I hope to travel tomorrow to Romen village. I have been invited by a friend to be part of an assignment. I will share some principles with you that I hope will be helpful."

Lah was anxious to hear the principles.

"Sharing these principles is one thing. Making use of them is another. I hope you will make use of them."

"I will try my best," Lah responded. "But how do we meet since you will travel?"

"Come here tomorrow morning before I leave. Our discussions after that will be on the phone."

"That's okay with me. I am curious to know the first principle."

"No matter how dark your situation is, you should never lose hope. Always believe that things can become better. This is the first principle."

Lah listened.

"There is no situation on earth, whether good or bad, that lasts forever. The opposite of good is bad and the opposite of bad is good. Each can lead to the other. There is a saying that 'every problem has an expiry date on it.'"

"I must confess that hope is the last thing I had before coming to you."

"Don't lose it. Problems are scared of hope."

"I am sure my time with you will be productive."

"A productive time is in the result, not in the recommendation. Ideas are orphans without the right applications."

Lah smiled.

"The first step towards progress often looks like an enemy, but it is a friend. Don't be afraid of it. Having the courage to take it leads you to other steps that are helpful in life."

"I am so comfortable listening to you that I don't want to go back home."

Nachau smiled. "Going back home is an indication of discovering a solution to the problem that pushed you out. Sometimes it takes courage to go back home. Not going back home shows me that you have not yet found courage."

"I agree with you. I will go back home."

"Thank you for your visit," Nachau said.

"I am grateful," Lah remarked.

^

"Since I can't get employment or sponsorship to further my education, I have decided to start a farming business. This will enable me to have resources to provide for the family and eventually go to school. I always feel that I can make things better for everyone in this village. I don't like the way my friends live. They need to stop wasting time at Mariban if they want to make progress. I will help them think well when I have the resources," Dimba said to his aged father, who lay on a mat under a tree, half paralyzed in the right hand and leg because of a stroke. Dimba was a hardworking, huge, tall and dark young man of twenty-seven years of age.

"That is a good idea, my son. I am proud of you. I am sure many people in this village also feel the same. You often think more of helping others. That is a good attitude. No matter what happens, don't lose it," Ntedu encouraged his son.

"Thank you, Papa."

"How do you expect to get the money to start the business?"

"I intend to share the idea with Uncle Eremale for his support."

Ntedu was quiet for a moment. His mood suddenly changed to sadness.

"Is anything the matter?"

"That is a good idea. Eremale has the money. He should be able to help you," Ntedu said, in an attempt to overcome his mood.

"I hope so. But I am worried over one thing."

"What is it?"

"Since uncle has the money, why has he failed to help us? At least you deserve to have been taken to a good hospital."

Ntedu kept quiet again.

"Did I say something that hurt you, Papa?"

"No, my son! You have only opened up an old wound. You reminded me of the good opportunities I misused in the past that made me dependent on people today instead of being strong to manage my family well."

"You have been mentioning this for some years, but you have never shared the story with me of what really happened," Dimba stated.

Ntedu looked up to the sky. "It is a long story. I will certainly tell you at the right time."

"I will wait for your right time that seems not to come."

"Don't let what I have said discourage you from meeting your uncle. Everyone has his time."

"I will meet him today in the evening."

"I wish you well."

Dimba was the only young man in Romen who was respected by both elders and some youth. Having come from a poor family, he was always willing to help himself without being a burden to anyone. His mother had died some years ago. Since then, the responsibility of caring for his father was laid on him and his sister, Suram, who was already married. She lived at Mari village not very far away from Romen. Dimba's friends in both Romen and Kiringa, who were much involved in irresponsible lifestyles, had tried to convince him to join them, but Dimba had remained committed to his conviction of achieving a better life for everybody in the village.

CHAPTER 2

At Mariban, many young people gathered as usual to drink their local beer. Ganduro also joined his friends, leaving his wife at home cooking.

"You are not supposed to be here until after one month of your marriage," Tani said jokingly.

Ganduro smiled. "There is nothing new. Have you forgotten that Yalami and I have been living together for some time before our marriage? I missed the company of friends and the pleasure of Mariban."

"I thought you would cling to your wife and forget about us! Now we know that friends are meant to stick together in all situations," Tani said.

All the friends laughed as they continued to tease Ganduro and sip beer.

"Good afternoon to you all," Dimba greeted the circle of friends, while passing along the road close to Mariban, which also led to his uncle's house.

The friends answered reluctantly.

"I didn't expect to see you here, Ganduro," Dimba stated.

Ganduro continued to drink his beer without uttering a word.

"Come and join us for a drink," Omem invited.

"Thank you. But why did you make the offer when you already knew my position on beer?"

"So, you still insist that we are the bad ones and you are the only good one?" Omem inquired in anger.

"I am not here for another argument on this matter. I only greeted you," Dimba calmly responded.

"Until you are ready to join us, we are not interested in your greetings!" Tani reacted harshly.

"Sorry for the interference," Dimba said, as he moved away towards his destination.

"He thinks he is better than us! He even had the courage to question me," Ganduro stated.

"Don't let him deny us the pleasure of Mariban. Forget about him and let us focus on our purpose for being here," Tani urged.

"Look over there," Ganduro said.

"What is it?" Tani asked.

"Calvin is coming in our direction," Ganduro informed them.

"I hope he won't come and disturb us about issues of life again? Let us respond to him with respect so that he will leave us alone," Tani advised.

When Calvin reached Mariban, he stopped. "How are you all doing?"

"We are doing fine, sir," Tani answered.

"Ganduro, how is your wife doing?" Calvin asked.

"She is fine," Ganduro replied gently.

"By the grace of God, I will visit you at home by 9am tomorrow, if you wouldn't mind," Calvin quickly stated.

"I will be pleased to see you, sir," Ganduro replied.

"Thank you. I wish you all well." Calvin moved away from them smiling because he knew he was not really welcome in their midst.

"You are in trouble," Omem said jokingly.

"He will not meet me at home tomorrow," Ganduro stated.

"What do you mean?" Tani remarked as he laughed.

"I will run away from home."

The friends laughed over Ganduro's response and concentrated on drinking the local beer.

Dimba was nervous when he got to his uncle's house. The thought of his uncle's probable response to his request preoccupied him. He stood at the gate for a few minutes thinking over how life could be better for him and others if his uncle would help him. The question of why his father was not helped by his uncle suddenly crossed his mind. He wrestled for a moment with it, but dismissed it with the conclusion that maybe his father had done something wrong to Eremale. Eventually, he summoned the courage and knocked at the gate. The gateman opened up and checked. He allowed Dimba in on seeing him. They greeted each other politely before Dimba asked after his uncle. The gateman informed him that his uncle was in.

Dimba went straight to the house. It was well built, with three expensive cars parked under a car shade. The garden looked well with well-maintained flowers and fruit trees among which birds sang.

Dimba knocked four times at the door, but there was no answer. He eventually gave up thinking that they were probably asleep. As he turned to leave, he suddenly heard footsteps heading towards the door from inside the building.

"Who is it?" Eremale, a tall man with a neatly shaved moustache asked.

"It is me, Dimba," he anxiously replied.

Eremale opened the door and smiled at Dimba. "You are welcome."

"Thank you, uncle."

"Come in."

They walked to the parlour and sat down. Dimba only became more nervous. The parlour was nicely decorated. Many things had changed since the last time he visited, which was a month ago.

"How is your father doing?" Eremale inquired gently.

"He is still struggling."

"I will try and see him tomorrow."

"How are your wife and Angela doing?"

"They are fine. My wife has gone to the market," Eremale replied. "Is there any problem?"

"I came to ask for your assistance," Dimba said calmly, after silence for awhile.

"What is it?" Eremale asked politely.

"Since I can't further my education now, I want to go into the farming business, especially dry season farming. This will enable me to have and save some money to further my education in the future. According to my plan, I would need a loan of sixty thousand Naira in order to start."

Eremale kept quiet for some time. Dimba anxiously waited for a reply.

"That is a very good idea. We are proud of you. You are not like your friends who waste time at Mariban drinking beer. I will help you to achieve your goal."

"Thank you, uncle!" Dimba said excitedly.

"I am the only uncle you have. If I don't help you, who else would do that?"

Dimba was smiling at his uncle's response.

Eremale was silent for a moment.

Dimba was in full expectation.

"However, you are really unlucky today. If you had come yesterday, I would have given you the money. I do not have money now because I bought a car yesterday with the whole of my savings. Nevertheless, you should come next week. I will see what I can do about it," Eremale explained.

Dimba smiled. "Next week is not very far off. I can wait."

"To be specific, you should come on Thursday by 8am."

"Okay."

"Take this and buy bread for yourself and your father. Tell him that I will see him tomorrow," Eremale stated, as he gave two hundred Naira note to Dimba.

"Thank you, uncle, for your kindness," Dimba said, while he stood up and walked out of the house.

On his way, he was grateful to God for his uncle's response. He had critically thought on why his father had earlier tried to portray a negative picture of his uncle. When he reached home, he gladly informed his father about the development, which made his father happy. As a support for his son, he took some money from underneath his bed and gave it to him to help him start the project.

"Where did you get the money from?" Dimba asked in surprise.

"Never mind. It is a long story."

"Thank you very much for the support. I promise you that I will make the best use of it. Surely, we will soon get out of poverty," Dimba stressed.

"I have no doubt about your ability to make good things happen," Ntedu responded with a smile.

"I will have the biggest farm in this village. People will come from far and near to buy from me," Dimba confidently said.

"I hope your uncle will keep to his word."

"I am sure he will. He was interested in the project. You needed to see how worried he was looking simply because he did not have the money today to give me."

"Let your confidence see you through."

"When I start the project, it will also challenge the young people in this village to give up idleness and drunkenness. They would also do better things with their lives for the development of themselves and the village."

"You have a good vision, my son. You are about to do what many of us were not able to do. If we had thought like you, we would not be suffering the way we do today," Ntedu said sadly.

CHAPTER 3

Calvin visited Ganduro's house as planned, but Ganduro was not in. Yalami was hospitable to him. As he returned to his compound, Calvin met the friends under a tree, smoking marijuana on the outskirts of the village.

"I am sure he is coming from my house," Ganduro said, while trying to hide.

"Hide behind the rock," Tani encouraged.

"We have the right to live the way we want. You don't have to hide," Omem commented.

"Good morning to you all," Calvin greeted with a smile when he reached them.

"Good morning, sir," they responded.

"Ganduro, I am coming from your house in regard to our appointment."

"Sorry, sir. I had forgotten that you were coming."

"That's okay. I met your wife. She is really a good woman. You should be proud to have her."

Tani looked at Ganduro and smiled jokingly. Omem also joined him in the smile as they expected a reply from Ganduro.

"Thank you for saying that about my wife."

"May I join you for some minutes?" Calvin requested.

"I don't think you can endure the odour of our environment," Tani stated.

"I have experienced worse in the past," Calvin remarked.

"You mean you also smoked marijuana?" Ganduro asked curiously.

"Yes. I also took cocaine," Calvin disclosed, as he sat down on a rock.

"I don't believe you, sir," Omem said.

Calvin smiled.

The friends continued to smoke as they stared at Calvin.

"I smoked at that time because of frustration. What about you?"

The friends kept quiet for a moment.

"I also smoke for the same reason," Tani replied.

"Me, too," Ganduro said.

"What about you, Omem?"

"I smoke because of my friends."

"You mean you don't like it?" Calvin asked.

"My father was an ex-service man. When he retired, we relocated to the village from the state where he had served. Here in the village, it was difficult for me to survive alone without smoking because most of the young people spent much time at Mariban. Eventually, in order to have friends, I had no choice, but join them," Omem explained.

The other friends angrily looked at Omem.

Calvin noticed the change of mood. "It seems you disagree with Omem."

"Who does he think he is?" Ganduro responded angrily.

"What do you have to say, Omem?" Calvin asked.

"I didn't say that to annoy anybody. I only answered the question you asked."

"You have no right to blame us over your situation!" Tani reacted.

"I will have to go now," Ganduro said.

"I will also go," Tani stated.

"You don't have to continue living this way. You can become better if you want to," Calvin quickly encouraged.

The three friends left Calvin sitting alone.

On the way, Ganduro and Tani spoke harshly against Omem, threatening never to associate with him again. Omem felt miserable over the situation. He repeatedly apologized for causing them pain. It took some time before he convinced them.

^

As arranged earlier, Lah visited Nachau. He was anxious to know the second principle. He was in a much better mood this time. He had spent a lot of time after their last discussions, thinking about what Nachau had told him and how he could start implementing the principle of hope. This time, he didn't want any single part of Nachau's speech to slip out of his memory. He came ready with a jotter and a pen to write.

The mango tree not far from where Nachau sat had some ripe fruits, very appealing to the eyes and appetizing too. Nachau had earlier plucked some mangoes from the tree. His wife, Akio, had washed them for him and served them in a plate, with a knife for easy eating. She had also brought some water in a basin and kept it beside him.

As Nachau sat alone, enjoying one of the mangoes, the gateman opened the gate and let Lah drive into the compound in a black car. He walked to Nachau the moment he got out of the car. Nachau washed his hand with the water in the basin. "You are welcome, Mr. Lah."

"Thank you."

"How is your family?"

"We are all fine. Your first principle has so far been helpful to me. Since yesterday, I have started seeing the world much more positively," Lah said, immediately he sat down.

Nachau smiled. "Hope helps you to see good in everything you face."

Lah listened.

"Have a mango, please."

"Not today, sir. Thank you for the offer," Lah said.

"I want us to discuss the first problem you mentioned, which is corruption," Nachau quickly stated. "People with negative point of view easily get involved in corruption, because they don't believe they can achieve success on their own. They are either hopeless people who are frustrated by past experiences, or have plans for the future which are bigger than their resources."

Lah nodded in understanding.

"Those people who have identified their potential are hardworking. They never rest until they solve the problems disturbing humanity. They add, they don't deny good things. They are motivated to keep going by the joy they bring into people's lives. They create resources and never live in fear of the day the resources might end, because they are always achieving more relevant things."

Lah wrote some points down quickly, as he concentrated on the next ones.

"In order to know those who are corrupt or have the tendency towards corruption, it is good to involve your staff in critical assignments. Ask each of them to write a short essay on what he or she could do to achieve a better future for himself, or herself, if he or she were not working in your company or not employed by anybody for the next ten years. Those who have good plans can be trusted more than those who haven't."

"I am glad I came to you."

"You should only be glad when these ideas work for you."

Lah smiled.

"Work with people who don't depend on you for their future. Those who depend on you fully are often afraid of losing their jobs. In view of that, they seize opportunities to enrich themselves so that at any time you dismiss them; they will not go empty handed."

"What motivates those who have good plans?" Lah quickly asked.

"Most of them are afraid of losing something in the future. They try to avoid making mistakes that will have negative consequences in the future and stop them from achieving their goals. They can become faithful managers today, not only because of you, but also because of themselves. They see your company only as a bus, conveying them to their destinations."

"Can we completely rule out the possibility of those with good future plans getting involved in corruption?"

"You should not rule out the possibility. We can't remove a problem one hundred percent, but we can minimize it. You will often need to remind those of your workers, who have shown you their personal plans, of where they are going. This helps to guide them on the right path."

Lah wrote more points in the jotter.

"Never work with any person who has not yet discovered a problem his life is meant to solve."

"Should I regard that as the second principle?" Lah inquired.

"Yes."

"I need more explanation."

"People who are not thinking of solving problems are thinking of creating them. Corruption is a problem that leads to many more problems."

Lah jotted down the second principle joyfully. "I feel like I am in school for the first time."

"Every day is an opportunity to learn; but learning becomes new and interesting when it deals with how to solve our problems," Nachau explained.

Lah smiled. "I think you are right. Thank you for your time once again. The second principle also makes sense to me."

"You are welcome. Don't forget that people fear the future because they are not prepared for it."

"I will prepare well today, to avoid corruption in my company," Lah stated.

"In everything we do, we should be like the first rain on the dry grass at the end of the dry season. Always refresh others as you refresh yourself. I hope these ideas will water your ideas for growth."

Lah smiled in confidence.

"Light bulbs become hot in projecting light. Bearing light always comes with some challenges. It is never a smooth journey. I wish you success."

"Thank you. I wish you a safe journey."

"I will expect your calls."

"Expect many of them," Lah said.

Nachau accompanied Lah to his car. On returning to pick his cell phone and get ready for the trip, the cell phone suddenly rang. On picking it, he saw the name of Kanem Pegulo, the person he met on a bus some years ago during his trip to Lagos. Kanem became a medical doctor and an author because of the discussions they had. His work had been successful. He had been in touch with Nachau since the first time they met.

"Hello, Kanem!" Nachau answered gladly.

"How are you, sir?" Kanem remarked excitedly.

"I am fine. How is your family?"

"We are doing well. How is yours?"

"I thank God."

"I called to inform you that I will come to the house in one hour by God's grace to pick you so that we can visit Calvin together. You don't have to use your car."

"That is a good idea. I am happy you now have the time for the trip."

"Serving God is the most important assignment in life, as you often say. I have to make time for it."

Nachau smiled. "I am glad you often remember that. Calvin will be glad to see both of us."

"The last time he called me, I perceived discouragement in the tone of his voice. He complained about the people's refusal to respond to the message, especially the young people," Kanem stated.

"I am happy he is beginning to feel discouraged."

"Why, sir?"

"Discouragement ends our personal efforts. It leads us to strength greater than our own," Nachau explained.

"I get your point. It is when a person is weak that he becomes strong."

"You are still the Kanem Pegulo I know," Nachau jokingly responded.

Both of them laughed over the statement.

"I will be on my way," Kanem said.

"I will be expecting you."

CHAPTER 4

Nachau and Kanem found the journey to visit Calvin challenging and interesting. The roads passed through various beautiful mountains and green hills. Cows were scattered over some hills, grazing under the watchful eyes of their shepherds. There was a major river in a village close to the road. Many children and adults were bathing in the river, while some fetched water from it using clay pots. Some animals also came to the river to drink. Suddenly, chaos erupted between human beings and animals.

The bridge built across the river was big, old and cracked in many parts. Animals were also crossing the bridge to the other side. The road was littered with cow dung. There had also been an accident on the bridge. A taxi driver had hit a motorcycle with his car. Neither the car driver nor the motorcyclist was injured, but the motorcycle was damaged. A security agent was there to take charge of the case.

Kanem had to horn repeatedly before he could find his way through the herd of cows in front of him. The cows had occupied the two lanes of the bridge. Bridge users had to move at their pace. The shepherds who were supposed to hasten the cows across the bridge were not bothered by the discomfort they were causing the other bridge users. They moved slowly, ignoring the complaints of many people.

Before Kanem realized it, he drove into a deep crack. It was by God's grace that he was able to avoid hitting the bridge and possibly falling into the river. Kanem was irritated over the situation the moment he was able to stabilize the car on the road. "I wonder what the government is doing with our taxes in this country. The lives of her citizens are often not considered!"

Nachau listened with concern.

"It would be cheaper to repair this bridge now rather than later!" Kanem complained.

"It will someday be better," Nachau said. "God will one day give us leaders that will have the courage and strong desire to say enough is enough to bad leadership."

"You strongly believe that, sir?"

"It is not easy to believe that; but I do."

"I am really looking forward to the time our leaders will be God-fearing, and will think more of making the country better than their pockets. Leaders that will not have sound sleep because they know that if they don't provide good roads, sound education, good health care facilities and other vital amenities of life; their citizens will live in frustration. Leaders who will be worried over the death of one person that is unknown to them because of lack of adequate medical attention, only because they read it in the newspapers."

"You really sound passionate about changing this country," Nachau said.

"As a medical doctor, the conditions I often see in many of our hospitals are pathetic. There are many patients, but few qualified medical workers. Where there are a reasonable number of medical workers, drugs are often said to be either insufficient or not available. I become worried whenever I see all these things," Kanem lamented.

"We are now in the dry season of our nation. It won't last forever, no matter how long it takes. A rainy season of positive leadership will one day come. A time is coming in this country, when bad leaders can't survive being bad, even if they have opportunities to do so. A time is coming when the people will be better and more organized than their leaders."

Kanem listened attentively.

"The bad leaders will no longer have people to use as they wish among their followers, because hardship will make the people wiser than their leaders. A time is coming, when money will cease to be the magnet for respect from people. A time is coming, when the children of the corrupt leaders, who have the money, but miss opportunities of learning through different experiences of life, will serve the children of the poor, who have no money, but have solutions to problems because of the challenges they have been dealing with. A time is coming when righteousness will prevail," Nachau emphasized.

"You speak like a Prophet, sir."

"That time will surely come, by the grace of God," Nachau assured him.

"I hope I will be around to see the time."

"Meeting you and Calvin on the bus to Lagos was part of the process. Calvin refused to rob the passengers on the bus because he had found a new road, and you returned to the village because you saw hope in change."

Kanem kept quiet for awhile thinking over what Nachau had said. His mind went back to their first meeting, which he remembered vividly. How he was cruel to people in his village and how he was banished. The thoughts of the people he had helped through his profession because he himself agreed to change also came to his mind. He also remembered the responses he had received from readers of his books. The truth of Nachau's words stared him in the face.

"Only changed people can change bad situations," Nachau remarked.

"So, many of our leaders often fail to bring about change because they are yet to experience it," Kanem stated.

"That is the point. A person who has experienced healing from a particular disease is more sympathetic with someone suffering from the same problem than a medical doctor who has never experienced it."

Kanem nodded in understanding.

Suddenly, they reached a checkpoint, where security agents stopped vehicles for routine checks. A blue van was in front of them. Nachau became attentive to see how the security agents would do their job.

When a security agent got to the driver of the van, the driver stretched out his hand and gave an amount of money to the security agent. Grabbing it quickly, the agent put it in his pocket and asked the driver to move on without checking the van's contents. Nachau was quick to observe that the amount given to the security agent was fifty Naira.

When the turn of Kanem and Nachau came for checking, the sound of a siren was heard coming from behind. The security agents became confused and commanded Kanem to drive his car off the road to enable the convoy approaching to pass easily. It was a big struggle for Kanem to do as he was commanded, in view of the narrowness of the road. One of the security agents shouted loudly to him to drive faster.

After the convoy of eight cars had passed, Nachau got out of the car and questioned the attitude of the security agent.

"Hello, sir," Nachau greeted.

"What do you want?" the security agent asked harshly.

"I want to talk to you," Nachau replied politely.

"Can't you see that I am busy?" the security agent asked.

"I won't take much of your time."

"What is it?" The security agent asked, as he wondered who Nachau could be. He told one of his colleagues to take over his post as he talked with Nachau. Kanem drove further on and pulled up, to enable other cars to pass easily.

"I am Nachau Turomale," Nachau introduced himself.

"I am listening," the security agent responded, while avoiding introducing himself.

Nachau was alert enough to see his nametag. "Renga, I am curious to know why you stopped us, but let the convoy pass without you doing your job?"

Renga was surprised at Nachau's mention of his name, but he suddenly realized that his nametag had betrayed him.

"They were important people," Renga replied harshly.

"How did you know that they were important people?"

"Only important people use that kind of siren and convoy," Renga explained.

"So, even criminals can pass your checkpoint safely, if only they can use a siren and the same convoy as the one that just passed?"

"What is your point?"

"We can never build this country successfully if we don't promote equality and respect for everyone. Since the convoy used a siren to pass easily shows how much they disregard your value and assignment here, which is to check all cars for security purposes. They did not even greet you. This means you are not important to them."

Renga listened attentively.

"In view of that, there was no need for you to be angry with us and shout at us the way you did."

Renga still listened.

"Everyone is important. The person you disregard today can help you become better tomorrow."

"You have a reasonable point. I will consider your advice," Renga calmly said.

"Thank you for listening," Nachau said, as he shook hands with Renga. "One more thing."

Renga gazed at Nachau in expectation.

"There was no need for you to accept the fifty Naira from the driver of the van."

Renga's face became gloomy as he pondered Nachau's penetrating remark.

"That fifty Naira may cost many people their lives and possessions because you don't know what he was carrying in the van."

Renga looked at Nachau in silence.

Nachau moved away to the car. He entered and they drove off.

Renga's colleagues came to him curious to know what Nachau had told him, but Renga dismissed them by telling them that he would inform them later.

After three hours of driving, Nachau and Kanem finally reached the village. Calvin and two members of his team, Japheth and Bwallam, welcomed them. It was a huge reunion for the three friends. Calvin's invitation to Nachau and Kanem was to assist him in the mission of helping the villagers understand the love of God. The mission would take them one to two months, depending on the need on the ground.

Nachau and Kanem called their respective wives and informed them of the safe trip. After three hours of discussions and rest, Calvin informed them to get ready to visit the Village Head for introductions. This proved to be an interesting visit. The Village Head welcomed them warmly. He prepared a local dish for them as part of the entertainment. While the food served them was strange and unpleasant to their taste, they knew that rejecting it would mean offending the Village Head. In acceptance of the new culture, they both prayed and ate the food with joy.

As they returned to Calvin's compound, which had three large huts, Nachau stood outside the compound appreciating the beautiful environment of the village, which was surrounded by high mountains, and a river close by. Even though it was dry season, grass grew close to the river. A vast land was there, but it was unused, despite its nearness to the river. Only signs of farms cultivated during rainy season were seen. Immediately, many ideas came to his mind, especially the possibility of dry season farming. He went into the compound and met Calvin and Kanem. "The strength of resources is not in their availability, but their being optimally harnessed for the good of all."

Calvin and Kanem looked at Nachau as they anticipated learning more from him.

"Unless people are first helped to know what they have and how they can use that to become better, it is difficult to break into their darkness, because darkness has walls and can form a city," Nachau remarked.

Calvin and Kanem nodded.

"There is a need for light here," Nachau said.

CHAPTER 5

Ganduro returned home drunk and met his wife in a sad mood. He sat down on a mat and asked for his food. Yalami kept quiet, her face looking as if she had never known a smile.

"Bring my food to me, woman!" Ganduro commanded.

Yalami did not utter a word.

"I am commanding you for the last time. Bring my food here!"

"Useful men work hard and bring foodstuff home for their wives to cook. You only spend your time drinking beer!" Yalami reacted.

"So, that means I am a useless man?"

"In fact, you are more useless than the most useless person I have ever seen!" Yalami responded bitterly.

"A good woman should have respect for her husband. I am sure you learnt this bad attitude from your mother. I will not end up like your father, who was caged by your mother!" Ganduro reacted, as he stood up with difficulty to approach Yalami.

"You are even lucky I married you despite your poverty. I am sure you will end up like your father, who was the worst drunkard in this village. You cannot abuse my parents and go free. You yourself know that our people are warriors and also hardworking. They are not afraid of anybody."

"I will slap you if you open your big, dirty mouth again!" Ganduro threatened.

Yalami shouted louder. "If you lay your hand on me, you will know the meaning of the saying that 'what a man can do a woman can do better.' Marrying you is the greatest mistake I have ever made. You have not been feeding me well since I came to this useless village of yours.'"

Ganduro slapped Yalami hard on her cheek.

"You slapped me!"

"What can you do?"

Yalami retaliated with a nasty slap on Ganduro's face. The two started hitting each other. Yalami got an edge over him, because of his being drunk, and threw him down. She sat on him and repeatedly hit him on his face with her hands. It took the concerted efforts of neighbours, who ran into the compound, to separate them.

In shame, Ganduro stood up, and looked at his wife, who stood ready to continue fighting. "We will know who the head of this house is. I don't want to see you here in the next thirty minutes."

"I am not afraid of you!" Yalami boasted.

Some of the older women rebuked Yalami, telling her to keep quiet.

"I will not keep quiet. Since this man married me, he has not been feeding me well. In my village, men take good care of their wives. When

I talked to him about that, he always responded by abusing my parents. Enough is enough. I don't know whether it is a taboo for you in this village to care for your wives?"

"Don't abuse our village," warned Bando, one of the men who had intervened to stop the fight.

"I will abuse this village and there is nothing you can do about it. Both elders and youth of this village lack a sense of right direction in life. The young people will only end up like their parents!" Yalami affirmed, while walking into the room to pack her things to go back to her village.

People stood in the compound murmuring because of what she had said. Ganduro's friends also rushed to the scene. When they heard what Yalami had said, they wanted to beat her up, but the elderly women stopped them.

Yalami came out of the hut with her bag, still insulting the people of Romen, as she moved out of the compound to Kiringa.

News went round Romen about the insults Yalami had rained on the people. The people were very angry with her. They were also ashamed of Ganduro for allowing a woman to defeat him in a fight. Ganduro walked head down in Romen, even though he blamed the influence of alcohol for his defeat. The Village Head also got to know about Yalami's insults. He was not happy with the development and hoped to investigate it further.

^

"You mean Ganduro said that about me?" Malena, Yalami's mother, a short, fat, and dark woman, who was 58 years old, reacted after hearing the story of her daughter when she reached home in tears.

"Ganduro and his people also teamed up against me and beat me up. I was lucky to escape without any injury," Yalami stated.

"I need to hear first from your husband before I take a position on the matter," Amsami, Yalami's father said. He is 63 years old, tall and slim. He was one of the advisers of the Village Head of Kiringa.

"What do you mean?" Malena responded with bitterness. "You are not using your senses well! There is no difference between you and Ganduro!"

Amsami looked on quietly.

"Has our daughter ever lied to us? Why must you not believe her now? Is it only from her stupid husband that you can hear the truth?"

"Say whatever you like. Until I hear from her husband, I will not believe only one side of the story," Amsami stated.

"That is why you can never achieve anything reasonable in your life!" Malena reacted.

"Yalami," Amsami called, ignoring his wife.

"Yes Papa?"

"You are going back to your husband's house today."

Yalami frowned in silence at her father's remark.

"Did you hear what I said?" Amsami asked.

Yalami still maintained silence.

"She is not going back to Romen. My daughter will stay here. There is nothing you or anybody can do about it!"

"We shall see who the head of the house is!" Amsami said.

"Papa, I will not go back to Romen. It is the last thing I will ever do! I cannot live without food. It is because you did not experience what I have experienced, that is why you are talking like that!" Yalami broke her uneasy silence.

Amsami was speechless for a short time, as he focused his attention on his daughter. "I hope you still remember that I am your father?" he said.

Yalami looked at her father anxiously.

"Then act as a good father, because a good father will never send his daughter into a lion's den," Malena remarked harshly.

Amsami stood up and quickly left the compound to avoid attracting neighbours.

"You cannot run away from this matter. You will come back to this house!" Malena said. "Yalami," she called.

"Yes Mama?"

"Go and put your luggage inside your room. We shall see who will send you back."

CHAPTER 6

Sleep was not easy for Nachau and Kanem. Mosquitoes disturbed them. They spent most of the night praying. As a result, they woke up by 8:30am. Nachau's phone rang immediately he woke up. When he picked it, he saw the name of Lah.

"Hello, Lah."

"Good morning, sir."

"Good morning. How are you doing?"

"I am doing better. I have been dialling your number for some hours since yesterday, but the network has been poor. How was your trip?"

"We arrived at the village in good condition. We met our friend doing well."

"I thought you went alone?"

"I went in company of a friend."

"I wish you well in your assignment."

"Thank you."

"I am really curious to know the next principle."

"Which problem do you want us to discuss today?" Nachau asked.

"Recently, members of the community where our refinery is located have been destroying our pipes. We have tried all possible means to reconcile our differences, but without success."

"What do you destroy as a result of what you are doing?"

Lah paused for a moment. "They said our work is polluting their river and farmlands."

"Since you used the word 'they,' it means the problem is not affecting you."

Lah kept quiet again, in deep thought.

"What is your opinion concerning what they said?"

"What they said is true," Lah responded reluctantly.

"Let us change it from 'they' to 'we.' The sentence will now be, 'We know that the nature of our work affects the farmlands and river of our host community,'" Nachau emphasized.

"That is how it should be," Lah quickly admitted.

"Have they also asked for compensation?"

"Yes."

"Asking is part of human nature. Needs that are not fulfilled can turn a good person into a murderer. In most cases, his victims are unknown. It is important you pay attention to them now before they fully pay attention to you later," Nachau clarified.

"What can we do to solve the problem?" Lah asked anxiously.

Nachau was quiet, thinking deeply.

"Hello, sir. Are you still there?"

"I am with you. The third principle is, love compensates better. People must first be convinced that you love them. You will never rest from their problems when compensation becomes a formal programme instead of a relationship. Always find ways of developing more informal relationships than formal ones."

"I need more explanation."

"There are two ways of relating with the people you compensate."

Lah was listening attentively.

"You either do things for them or do things with them. The central focus before compensation is the existence of a problem. People love those who share their problems, because there are deep thoughts, expressions of genuine love and development in sharing. A crisis is easier managed when it becomes our crisis instead of their crisis.

Lah nodded in understanding.

"When you want to assist people, don't always approach them as a community, because some people will still not benefit. Such people can also rise up against you in the future."

"Okay."

"You should once in awhile use the method of reaching them as individuals or families."

Lah listened attentively.

"Do you live among them? Do you drink the water they drink? Do you depend on farmlands and river the way they do?"

"No."

"Then you can't understand them when they cry."

"You are making me feel guilty."

"I am only challenging you to think. Always avoid the mosquito-approach to humankind. They take the blood, and infect us with a disease."

Lah was glued to his cell phone. He was speechless, as he pondered the kind of person Nachau was.

"Are you still there?"

"I am, sir. You have succeeded in making me restless. For the first time, I am beginning to see things from the perspective of our host community."

"Perspectives depend on the motive to function well. You will never see what you don't want to see. What would be your target if you were a drop of rain with only one chance to touch the ground?"

"I would ensure that I refresh at least one plant."

"Go and do likewise with your host community, because now is the time you have. Do whatever good you can do now, not tomorrow, because tomorrow is real only to those who live to see it."

"But we are not sure of meeting all their demands. They are demanding a lot from us, that is the main problem."

"If your father was an authorized hunter and killed an elephant, would you go to him with the same size of basin that you would use when he killed an antelope?"

Lah was quiet again, thinking deeply. "No," he replied.

"Why?"

"The meat of an elephant is of much larger quantity than that of an antelope."

"The same principle applies to your host community. They know what you get from their lands. The determinant of their demands is the bulk of your income."

Lah listened.

Nachau waited for him to talk.

"I am grateful to you for challenging me to think better. Now I know what to do."

"I wish you well. Always remember that life is friendly to people who know its secrets."

"Thank you once again. I will call tomorrow."

"I will wait for your call."

After the discussions with Lah, Nachau got out of bed and brushed his teeth. Breakfast was already prepared. Kanem, Calvin, Japheth and Bwallam were discussing when Nachau joined them. They had earlier eaten their breakfast. They all greeted him and invited him to join them on a mat to eat his breakfast. Nachau gladly replied to their greetings and joined them. They served him bread and tea. He prayed and ate happily.

"How far have you got with your mission work?" Nachau asked Calvin.

"Not too far. It has really been challenging."

"How are you coping with the pastor you earlier told me about?"

"He is still fighting us. We are trusting God to reach his heart."

"There is no heart that is invincible to God. We could meet him for a discussion," Nachau suggested.

"I hope he will grant us audience," Calvin responded without confidence.

"Never underestimate what God can do," Nachau said.

Calvin nodded.

"What about the people?" Nachau asked.

"The people are still stubborn towards the message. They are lazy, and are not willing to work hard to help themselves. They want things for free, and when you don't give them what they want, they become angry and reject you," Calvin explained.

"What are the values of their culture?"

"Their main values are idol worship, territorial protection and communal living," Calvin explained.

"How have you been relating with them?" Nachau inquired further.

"I try to find 'common ground' between them and us, and lead them from what they know to what they don't know."

"Have you ever tried the project method?" Kanem asked, as he joined the discussions.

"We have not yet reached that stage," Calvin explained.

"That is a good question, Kanem," Nachau commended.

Kanem smiled in response.

"Do you have any project in mind?" Calvin inquired.

"I would use my training as a medical doctor to help the people become better," Kanem answered.

"How do you hope to do that?" Calvin asked further. "We don't have medical facilities in Romen. The people have often depended on traditional solutions. Only Kiringa has a local clinic."

"Excuse me," Kanem said, as he stood up and walked to his car. On getting there, he removed a big green bag, and brought it to his colleagues. "Now we have it! We will create a health centre," he stated, while opening the bag.

To the surprise of his colleagues, they saw that it was filled with different types of medicine and diverse portable medical equipment.

"I knew it would come to this stage, so I was prepared for the trip," Kanem explained.

Nachau looked excitedly at Kanem. "That is why I told you that the time for change in this country has started. People who think about the needs of others even before the people realize them are greatly needed in this nation."

Kanem smiled. "Everyone has something to offer."

Calvin also smiled. "I am glad to have you people here."

Japheth and Bwallam only looked at the friends in excitement.

"We could also reach them through their stomach. It is easier to reach the stomach than to reach the heart," Nachau stated.

"How do you intend to do that?" Calvin inquired anxiously.

"I observed that Romen is blessed with vast land and a river close by, but the people don't seem to utilize the potential of dry season farming. They can get sufficient crops for domestic consumption and commercial purposes from it," Nachau explained.

"As I said earlier, the people are too lazy to work. Most of the young men only spend their time in a place called Mariban, where they take local beer. Only one young man called Dimba is thinking about a bright future. How do you deal with the laziness of the people?" Calvin asked.

"We could give them reasons for hard work. Someone said that 'man's greatest motivation is his personal interest,'" Nachau clarified.

Kanem nodded in understanding. "I still remember my mother's proverb, which says 'with the right approach, a young goat can suck a hyena's breast.'"

"The hyena must first be a God-fearing one before that happens," Calvin responded jokingly.

All of them laughed over the comments of Kanem and Calvin.

"A man becomes restless when he is exposed to new ways of doing things. As a result, his curiosity is stimulated and he searches for answers to his new questions. Eventually, he becomes an advocate of his new discoveries," Nachau said.

"How do we start?" Calvin asked, after thinking for awhile.

"We will start with the Village Head, by partnering with him to enable him to own a dry season farm," Nachau disclosed.

"I am sure the Village Head will like the idea, because he has been complaining bitterly over the laziness of his people," Calvin stated.

"We can sponsor the whole farm project for him," Kanem suggested.

"It is a good idea, Kanem, but at this stage, it will make him depend on us. As a start, let us help him to help himself and his village in order to be independent of us in future. There is a saying that, 'you teach a person how to fish, instead of fishing for him,'" Nachau explained.

Kanem smiled in understanding.

"We shall see the Village Head tomorrow by God's grace to discuss the two ideas of the medical centre and the farming project. It is better we use today for prayer and waiting on the Lord for further guidance," Calvin stated.

"Prayer is very important," Kanem commented.

"I also support the idea," Nachau remarked.

Calvin smiled. "Japheth, please take this bag to their room."

^

At Mariban, Ganduro met with his friends. "I curse the day I saw Yalami. I curse even more, the day I married her. I will never advise even my enemy to marry a woman from Kiringa."

"You are a man. There is no condition that you cannot handle. Forget about Yalami. I can't understand what came over you in the first place to marry a girl from Kiringa," Tani commented.

"I thought beer is a friend. However, this time, it has let me down. The shame of being defeated by a woman will disturb me for the rest of my life. Even children laugh at me in Romen," Ganduro reacted worriedly.

"There is no need to hate yourself. Beer is still our friend. It is just that it was not helpful at that moment," Omem remarked.

"My mother wants me to go to Kiringa and bring my wife back. She has been disturbing me over it."

"What is your opinion about your mother's demand?" Tani eagerly asked.

"I am confused. Right now I don't know the best decision to take!"

"You will be a fool if you bring Yalami back to your house. Forget about her and let us enjoy life together. You can find another wife in Romen whenever you are ready. Don't let your mother live your life for you," Tani emphasized.

Ganduro was quiet.

"I completely support what Tani said. Your wife didn't even respect us as your friends. The first time we visited you after the wedding ceremony, she didn't even give us water to drink!" Omem said in anger.

Ganduro picked a calabash of beer and drank it all. He stood up and quietly started moving away from his friends.

"Where are you going?" Tani asked.

Ganduro turned, and looked at him in confusion. "I am going to kill myself!"

Tani and Omem quickly stood up, grabbed him and brought him back to his seat. "Don't die today. We still need you," Tani said, as he laughed in mockery of Ganduro.

"This world is terrible!" Ganduro lamented.

"Don't die because of a woman. Your funeral will not be interesting," Omem teased.

"You can never understand my situation. You only open your big mouths to talk."

Tani and Omem laughed louder.

Ganduro stood up and went away from Mariban.

"Please, don't kill yourself. The beer at Mariban is still sufficient for all of us," Tani mocked Ganduro the more.

^

Nachau, Kanem and Calvin went to see pastor Namo for discussion. On getting there, they met him sitting under a tree reading the Word of God. He was not happy to see Calvin, but he struggled not to show his anger. "You are all welcome," Namo said.

"Thank you," the friends answered.

Namo called one of his daughters to bring some wooden chairs for his guests. The girl hurried to do as she had been told. Calvin and friends sat down and greeted Namo happily. Calvin took some time to introduce his guests and their purpose in coming to Romen. "We are here to discuss further with you on our mission in Romen, and to once again seek for your partnership," Calvin stated.

Namo nodded in silence.

"I am sure, as I often told you, that God brought us here so that we could work together," Calvin said.

"Thank you for coming," Namo interrupted quickly. "I understood you well on our first discussion. I still reaffirm that when God called me, I clearly heard Him say that He has given me Romen to win for Him, and establish a Church. How can He then call another person to the same place?"

Nachau, Calvin and Kanem listened attentively.

"That is why I will never believe you when you claim that God has sent you to Romen," Namo emphasized.

"Don't forget that God uses different people at different times and in different ways. I don't think there is any issue of confusion here. You cannot do the work alone. The hand in the body should not reject the leg; both need each other," Calvin explained politely.

"I still maintain my position," Namo insisted.

"May I come in at this point?" Nachau asked.

Namo looked at Nachau quietly for awhile. "You can say what you want to say!"

"We are grateful to God for the opportunity to discuss with you. Calvin had been sharing with us your views about his presence here. I am happy about your passion in serving God. I hope the Lord will bless your efforts in line with His perfect will."

"Amen," Namo replied reluctantly.

"If you would not mind, I would like to ask you a personal question," Nachau requested.

"Go ahead," Namo approved calmly.

"How many children do your parents have?"

"Six."

"Are you the firstborn?"

"Yes."

"I pity the younger ones, because I guess you don't like them," Nachau remarked.

"Why did you say that?"

"The way you explained God's call to you to Romen as the first person, shows that you think God approves of only the first, not the second."

Namo kept quiet as he stared at Nachau.

"If you love the younger ones in the family, then you must transfer that love to us as the second people God has called to this place. The whole idea of God's ministry is to build a family that will be effective for His kingdom."

Namo silently bowed his head, thinking for a moment.

"We are only tools in God's hands. The work is His own not ours. He has equipped us with different gifts so that we can benefit from each one, working as a team. Our task is to mobilize people for change, while yours is to nurture them to maturity in Jesus," Nachau explained.

Namo listened attentively.

"A story is told of 'the shortest tree in a forest which grows on tall mountains. As a result, it becomes the tallest tree in the forest.' The nature of the mountain has helped the tree to achieve what it could not have achieved alone. That is what partnership does to people who cherish it," Nachau clarified.

Namo was still quiet.

Nachau and friends waited patiently for him to speak.

"I have never looked at it from your point of view," Namo remarked.

"Every right time has its right lenses," Nachau stated.

"I will think over what you said," Namo responded calmly.

"We would certainly wait for your feedback," Nachau said.

They prayed together, and eventually Nachau and his friends went back to their mission house in confidence that God had answered their prayer.

CHAPTER 7

Early in the morning, about 3:30 am, Lah called Nachau. When Nachau woke up and saw the call, he smiled at Lah's anxiety. "Good morning."

"Good morning, sir. I know I have disturbed your sleep; but I ask that you listen to me for a few minutes. I am sure you understand that curiosity is not a good pillow."

"Don't worry, I certainly understand. I will call after fifty minutes, to enable me to have my devotion," Nachau said.

"Okay."

"Thank you for understanding me."

"I am the one to thank you."

Following an encouraging devotion, Nachau called Lah. When Lah answered, he asked Nachau to end the call to enable him to call back.

"Let me burn the units today."

"I insist on burning the units, for I am the one with the problem," Lah emphasized.

"A person with a problem needs help. What is the problem for today?"

Lah kept quiet as he thought about Nachau's attitude.

"Are you still with me?"

"I am with you. The next problem is the destruction of two of our offices in the past by some angry youths. Lives and possessions were lost because of that."

Nachau listened.

"We are now living in fear. How can we handle this?"

Nachau kept quiet for a moment, while Lah waited in anticipation.

"This leads us to the next principle. Happy people don't destroy progress. Anger must first reach the explosive stage before destruction is carried out.

Lah listened attentively.

"Violent reactions are like letters that need to be read and understood. They show that people are angry with you, either because your activities are against their belief system or they are frustrated because of what you refuse to do to help them achieve their personal or collective goals," Nachau explained.

Lah listened.

"Wisdom is the ultimate in managing crises. The crisis you manage with wisdom hardly ever gives birth to other crises. "

"How can I get and apply the right wisdom?" Lah quickly inquired.

"You get it from God. He is the only source of true wisdom."

Lah listened well.

"There are two things I want you to do."

"I am listening," Lah replied eagerly.

"You should first take the list of people you are sure are angry with you. The second list should be of those you think are not happy with you. Commit them to God in prayer, asking Him for guidance on how to reach them before they reach you again."

"Is the use of force okay if peaceful means do not work?"

"It is only when you see a target that you can hit it rightly."

Lah listened.

"Frustration and belief systems are the two main causes of violence. In order to eradicate the frustration you need to locate its root causes. Belief systems are much more difficult to deal with. To change them you need to work with ideas and 'values, rather than their outward forms.'"

"What do you mean?"

"Which one of these two causes bitterness: renovating a person's house or ejecting him from it?"

"Ejecting him," Lah immediately answered.

"You got it right."

Lah was quiet, thinking deeply over the discussions.

Nachau was also quiet in expectation.

Lah was still quiet.

"If you don't have more questions, then we will continue the discussion another time."

Lah was still quiet.

"Lah," Nachau called.

"Yes sir."

"I will allow you to think over the discussions."

"Thank you, sir. I will certainly call again."

Nachau went back to sleep for some minutes. Later, he left his hut and stood outside the compound admiring the beautiful scenery of the village. The sun was rising, and the river was calm. It was really a wonderful sight to admire. The sound of cocks crowing was heard repeatedly.

Soon afterwards, Calvin, Kanem, Japheth and Bwallam also came out of their huts. Nachau went back to the compound, and together with his colleagues had their collective devotion. They also discussed how they would approach the Village Head and discuss the proposed farm and clinic projects. Eventually, they were all comfortable with the outcome of their discussions.

Nachau picked his cell phone and called his wife, finding out their situation at home. Kanem also did likewise. They were both happy to hear that their families were doing well.

Later that morning, they went and had a successful discussion with the Village Head. They were greatly encouraged and motivated by his acceptance. He promised them full support and partnership, to ensure the success of the projects.

As part of the preparations for his investment, Dimba used the money his father gave him to hire more hands to help him clear the farmland his mother had given him before her death. The land was close to the river and very fertile. He was hopeful that his uncle would later be proud of him, because of the way he would manage the resources he hoped to get from him.

Tani and Omem heard of the project and came to see it for themselves. They met Dimba and others working hard.

"Well-done, Dimba," Tani said, as they approached him.

"Good morning to you all," Dimba replied casually, while focusing on his work.

"We can see that your farm project is progressing," Omem stated.

"Yes," Dimba replied confidently. "Very soon, we will attain commendable results; but for now, there is a lot of work to be done," he responded, as he left the work to focus on his visitors.

"We learnt that you are planning to start dry season farming, that is why we came to see it for ourselves," Tani said.

"Dry season farming is a good project. I believe very much in its potential. Our land is fertile and the river is close to us with sufficient water. If only we can use our resources well, I am sure we can reduce poverty in our village and open the way for development. We have a duty to do better than our parents in this regard," Dimba explained,

"It has never been done in this village. What makes you so sure that the idea will work?" Omem asked doubtfully.

"I saw it the last time I visited Mari. Since it worked for them, there is no reason for it not to work here," Dimba explained confidently.

Both Tani and Omem laughed over Dimba's explanation. "Now I know why you always refuse to join us at Mariban," Tani commented.

"Only activities that will make us better are worth focusing on. I have a burden of creating a better village for every one of us," Dimba responded.

"In other words, you believe that all of us who spend time at Mariban are useless," Omem quickly remarked.

"That is not the point. What makes you feel satisfied may not be the same as mine. In life, everybody has a choice," Dimba said.

"How do you intend to get money to fund your project? I am sure it will not come from your father," Tani remarked in mockery.

"What is wrong with my father, that you think he cannot help me with money?"

"I only thought of his condition. It would be better to raise some money and take him to the hospital rather than wasting it on this project of yours," Tani advised.

"Please, if you wouldn't mind, I need to focus on my work," Dimba said.

"That means you are sending us away because we told you the truth!" Tani remarked.

"If you don't get out of here, I will use this hoe to show you the nature of my anger!" Dimba reacted furiously.

"Do your worst, if you think you are a man!" Tani challenged.

Dimba raised his hoe high to hit Tani on the head, but luckily, Tani dodged being hit. Suddenly, Tani realized that Dimba had really meant to carry out his threat.

"You are mad!" Tani said bitterly.

"You will end up like your father!" Omem cursed Dimba.

Dimba chased them, but they outran him to safety, cursing as they fled. No sooner had he returned than one of the people working for him advised him on anger management. Still angry, Dimba continued his work without uttering a word.

CHAPTER 8

Dimba was very happy because the moment to meet his uncle about the money had come. He was neatly dressed with a red shirt on top of white trousers. His black sandals were well polished.

On reaching his uncle's house, the gateman welcomed him. Dimba went and knocked at the door. The uncle's daughter, Angela, came and opened the door. She was seventeen years old, tall and light in complexion.

"You are welcome."

"Thank you."

"Please, come in."

Dimba walked in and sat on a chair. The situation in the house sent him a signal that only Angela was home. "Is uncle at home?" he quickly asked.

"No. Daddy and Mummy travelled to Mari early in the morning."

"Did he leave any message for me?" Dimba asked anxiously after a short silence.

"He didn't. Did he give you any appointment?"

"Yes. He told me to come today, by this time."

"They will be back in the afternoon by 1pm. You should come back by 2pm," Angela said.

"I will do just that."

Dimba bowed his head in frustration when he left the house. Several thoughts came to his mind on why his uncle forgot the appointment. He comforted himself with the fact that maybe he had not forgotten.

Later in the afternoon, Dimba returned and knocked. Once again, Angela opened the door. She informed him that her father was at home. He entered the parlour and sat down. Angela asked Dimba to wait because her parents were resting in their room.

Angela served a cup of water to Dimba. The waiting lasted for more than two hours before his uncle finally woke up and came out of his room. When Eremale came to the parlour and saw Dimba, he reluctantly welcomed him after exchanging greetings.

"Angela told me that you came in the morning," Eremale said, while sitting down.

"Yes Uncle. How was your trip?"

"We came back safely," Eremale responded, as he picked a newspaper on the centre table to read.

"I came in regard to our last discussion."

"I have not forgotten," Eremale said after a short silence.

Dimba kept quiet in expectation.

"It is very unfortunate that I still don't have money. Your cousin, Angela, insisted that she needed her own car. I had no option, but to get it for her. There is an amount of money I have been expecting. Up till now I have not gotten it," Eremale explained, while reading the newspaper.

Dimba could not believe his ears. He immediately started having various discouraging thoughts.

Suddenly, the cell phone of Eremale rang. He picked it and hurriedly excused himself and went out.

"Hello, my dear," Monica, one of Eremale's concubines, said.

"I thought I told you not to call me by this time."

"Sorry, my love. It is just that I am in desperate need."

"If you continue like this, you will get me into trouble with my wife," Eremale remarked in a low tone.

"Don't worry, she will never know. Be a strong man," Monica said seductively.

"What do you want?"

"I need more money to take care of some needs."

"What happened to the one hundred thousand Naira I gave you two days ago?"

"I am sure you know that one hundred thousand Naira is not enough to take care of the needs of a good woman for two days. You know without you, I have nobody," Monica emphasized.

Eremale smiled in response. "How much do you need?"

"One hundred and fifty thousand Naira only will be enough for now."

"Give me some minutes. I will drive to town and meet you."

"Are you coming with the money?"

"Don't worry. I am sure you know that one hundred and fifty thousand Naira is not a big deal to me," Eremale boasted.

"I will prepare your favourite dish before you come," Monica stressed.

"You are making me feel like rushing to your place right now."

"That is your decision to make," Monica said seductively.

"Till I come."

"I am already expecting you."

After the discussions, Eremale went inside the parlour and joined Dimba. "As I earlier said, I don't have money now. You can go home. When I get the money I am expecting, I will send for you to come," he said, while sitting down.

Dimba was furious in his mind because he had overheard his uncle's conversations on the phone. He knew that Eremale had the money, but didn't want to support him. He stood up slowly and went out of his uncle's house without saying a word. Eremale called him to take two hundred Naira as a gift, but Dimba did not look back.

Dimba's walk back home can be described as the journey of the lost. His imagination had gone wild, trying to figure out the best solution to his problem. Tears rolled down his cheek as he thought over how greedy people like his uncle could be; preferring their personal interest to the interest of others. The thought of changing his lifestyle to deal with his uncle severely for his selfishness crossed his mind. Suddenly, he tripped over a stone and his sandal developed a problem. He stood there for some minutes, thinking about his situation. As a solution, he removed the sandal and held it with his hand, as he walked home. On his way, he saw Tani, Ganduro and Omem at their usual spot, under a tree on the outskirts of the village, smoking marijuana. He approached them gently.

"Look over there, the farmer is approaching us," Omem alerted them.

"Let us not say a word to him. He is a wicked person. He thinks we are useless," Tani said.

The moment Dimba came to them, he sat on a stone in their midst without saying a word to any of them. His face showed his disappointment. Instead of bitterness towards him, Tani, Omen and Ganduro became curious to know the reason for his face being gloomy.

"Can I have what you are smoking?" Dimba calmly requested.

"It is marijuana," Ganduro answered in confusion.

"I know. I want you to teach me how to smoke it."

"What has happened to you? You looked as if the world has fallen on you," Tani stated.

"You were right to ask me where I would get funding for my project. My uncle promised me some money. Eventually, he didn't keep his promise even though he has the money to support me!" Dimba explained.

"Welcome to our world," Omem said.

"Our stories are similar to yours. It is just that you never asked us why we do what we do," Tani commented after silence for a short time. "We were also disappointed in one way or the other by the people we knew could help us."

"People like my uncle must pay for their greed!" Dimba reacted.

"There are many of them in this village," Omem remarked bitterly.

"We should make them notice us by giving them rough justice," Dimba roared in anger.

"What do you have in mind?" Ganduro inquired.

"Since our asking did not yield any good fruit, our use of force can," Dimba explained.

"I am with you on this," Tani said.

"I am also in," Omem agreed.

"My life has already crumbled. I have nothing to lose. I am also in," Ganduro stated.

"Give me marijuana," Dimba demanded.

Omem gave him his marijuana. Dimba rushed at it. Suddenly, he started coughing heavily with tears in his eyes.

"Don't worry, you will get used to it soon," Tani encouraged.

"I am glad you are now on our side," Omem said.

Dimba only nodded, as he tried to get used to the odour and inhaling of marijuana.

As the friends spent their time smoking and developing their master plan of response to the greedy people, Calvin and Kanem approached them.

"Calvin is coming," Omem announced.

"He is coming to disturb us, again," Tani stated.

"To avoid being disturbed, you need to stay silent no matter what he says," Dimba advised.

When Calvin and Kanem reached the friends, they greeted them, but they stayed silent. Calvin was surprised to see Dimba smoking marijuana. He then knew that something terrible had happened.

"Can we sit with you for awhile?" Calvin asked.

"No, we don't need your company," Tani quickly reacted.

"This is my friend, Kanem, from the city," Calvin said, ignoring Tani's reaction.

"You are welcome," Omem remarked.

"Thank you," Kanem shook hands with Omem.

"You are welcome, sir," Ganduro stated.

Kanem smiled and shook hands with Ganduro.

"You are welcome to our village," Tani said reluctantly.

"Thank you," Kanem remarked.

"Ganduro, I went to your house when I heard of what happened between you and your wife, but I did not meet anybody home. I hope you and your wife will find a good solution to the problem," Calvin stated.

Ganduro kept quiet.

"Dimba, you are also here?" Calvin asked curiously.

"What does that mean?" Dimba reacted harshly.

"Sorry, if my question has offended you," Calvin replied. "But I am sure you know what I meant."

"I am no longer the Dimba you used to know!"

"Would you be willing to share your challenge with me? Maybe I can be of help," Calvin quickly responded.

Dimba stood up and hurried away angrily.

Tani, Ganduro, Omem, Calvin and Kanem looked at him as he moved away.

"I am scared at what Dimba might do," Calvin said.

"He is beginning to scare us too," Tani stated.

"Was he the Dimba you told us about?" Kanem inquired.

"Yes," Calvin answered.

When Dimba got home, his father was lying on a mat, resting. Before speaking to him, Dimba entered his room to calm himself. Noticing Dimba's mood, his father became curious. He called him four times before he responded. He came out weeping in anger, as he approached his father.

"I am sure your uncle has disappointed you," Ntedu said.

Dimba was wiping his tears with the edge of his shirt, while weeping the more without saying a word to his father.

"Sit down close to me, and let us talk."

Dimba sat down on the mat. "You knew that Eremale would disappoint me, yet you still gave me your support to start the land preparation for the business."

"You smell of marijuana," Ntedu said worriedly.

"That is not the point. You should answer my question!"

Ntedu became silent for a moment.

"It is very important that you answer my question!"

"I knew he would disappoint you. He loves disappointing his extended family members. I wanted you to find that out for yourself."

"I need to know what happened between you and him."

"It is a long story, but I will just get to the point."

Dimba listened carefully.

"Eremale and I as you know are the only surviving children of our parents. When our parents died, I dropped out of school to take care of Eremale. I was the one that sponsored him in school to university level. Eventually, he abandoned me when he started getting money. That is why neither I nor any of you enjoys his wealth," Ntedu narrated.

"He must pay back your investment in him. He can't go free!" Dimba responded furiously.

"There is nothing we can do about that now. Past is past. We need to find new ways of surviving and creating wealth for ourselves. I am worried because I don't want to die and let you and your sister inherit my poverty."

"Papa, there is nothing you can do, but there is something I can do. I will show Eremale that a greedy person has no right to live in this village."

 Ntedu kept quiet, looking at Dimba.

"A man is supposed to reap what he sows. Since Eremale chose to sow bitterness, then bitterness shall he reap!"

"Don't do anything that you will regret later," Ntedu cautioned.

"I will never regret anything, because I don't have anything to lose!"

"Your uncle is rich. He can outsmart you if you try to harm him."

"There are many things his money cannot do for him!"

"You have options at your disposal, but only do what is right."

Dimba kept quiet, thinking over his plan of action to teach Eremale a lesson he would never forget.

CHAPTER 9

Lah called Nachau the next morning for the next principle.

"I hope you have been thinking of effective applications for the principles we have discussed?" Nachau asked after they greeted each other.

"Yes sir."

"That is good, because someone said that 'knowledge without right application is like an abortion.'"

"In my situation, I will not experience an abortion."

Nachau smiled. "What is the next problem you want us to discuss today?"

"The unproductivity of most of my workers," Lah disclosed.

"How do you employ them?" Nachau asked thoughtfully.

"We use ethnic quotas in order to balance our diversity in the company."

"Do you consider formal educational qualifications?"

"It is the highest consideration, followed by work experience."

Nachau kept quiet while he thought deeply.

Lah waited anxiously.

"The next principle is those with informal education also have solutions to our problems."

Lah listened.

"Employment based on ethnic quotas is a weak argument. You will never have the results you need when you emphasize it more than competence. People will often promote the interests of their ethnic groups first, before the interests of your company."

Lah listened attentively.

"Your main focus on educational qualifications for employment is good, but it is not the only solution. It disqualifies those who only have informal education, but have the potential to take your company to greater heights."

"I am listening carefully."

"Our world has often succeeded in limiting solutions to those with formal education. There are many solutions wasting away on the streets among those we often prevent from contributing to development. They are aware that we don't want them, and because of that, they keep their opinions to themselves."

Lah picked a pen and jotter and wrote the ideas down quickly.

"A story is told of 'a man who had a flat tyre outside of a town, close to where a madman lived. After removing the tyre and replacing it with the spare tyre, he realized that some bolts were missing. He became confused, not knowing what to do to solve the problem. The madman came to him and said, 'Sir, remove one bolt from each of the other three tyres and you will have three bolts to fix this one with. When you get to town, you should buy more bolts.' When the man tried the advice of the madman, it worked for him."

Lah smiled. "The madman was indeed very clever."

"I agree with you; but who would expect that from a madman?"

"I must admit that I would not expect anything good from a madman."

"I hope the story will make you change your mind?"

"Certainly, sir."

"We sometimes get qualified staff, but not effective ones."

"I am happy I came to you."

"I am glad you are willing to learn."

Lah smiled.

"I want to also comment on the high consideration experience is given in employment. To me, it is a weak argument. 'How did the first workers in the world get their jobs?' If we do not employ fresh people, what happens when those with experience are phased out? The new people need to work first in order to become the next experienced people you are looking for. The people you give job experience to are often more loyal to you than those that came in with their experiences."

"Those with formal educational backgrounds and job experiences make the jobs easier."

"Which one do you prefer: an easy working system or a result-oriented system?"

"A result-oriented system."

"When people are running after a thief, and suddenly a man catches the thief, will the people ask the man for his qualifications or security experience? Will they not cheer him for solving a problem? The major aim of working is to solve humanity's problems. In view of that, only people who help us solve our problems should be observed, tested, and employed," Nachau emphasized.

"I get your point."

"Those we throw out for lack of formal educational qualifications often turn around and work against us and the systems we have created."

"When those with informal education are given such attention, won't that deprive them of the desire for formal education?"

"Let me assure you of a class of people, who can shun the formal education on their doorway. Those who want to study will study in spite of whatever challenges or encouragement you give them."

"Thank you once again. I have understood you well.

"You are welcome. I am happy because you understood me well."

^

After discussing his idea with Nachau and Calvin to help Dimba, Kanem went to see Dimba at home. On getting to the house, he met Dimba on his way out. Dimba was reluctant to respond when Kanem greeted him.

"I hope you can still remember me?"

"You are a friend of Calvin."

"Now, I am also your friend."

Dimba kept quiet.

"Calvin said a lot of good things about you. I was surprised to see you smoking marijuana the last time we met."

Dimba remained quiet, as he bowed his head.

"Can we sit on that stone?" Kanem asked, pointing to a stone close by.

"I am in a hurry. My friends are waiting for me. You were lucky to have met me at home. I have to care for my father's needs."

"I won't take much of your time."

Dimba looked at Kanem in silence.

"Is your father in?"

"Yes."

"Let us go in so that I can greet him."

They went into the compound and Kanem greeted Dimba's father. When they came out, they sat on the stone.

"Who has disappointed you?"

"What do you mean?"

"Who made you angry?"

"Nobody," Dimba responded, after contemplating Kanem's question. He was thinking about Kanem's sensitivity in understanding the cause of his actions. "How did you know of my situation?"

"Some years ago, I was in your situation. Disappointed by most of the people I trusted, including my father. You are not alone in this world, my friend."

Dimba paused in silence for some seconds. "My uncle built my hope so high, and later destroyed it. In view of that, I made a vow that he must pay for his selfishness."

Kanem smiled. "What did you ask him to do for you?"

"I went to him with a project proposal and asked him for a loan of sixty thousand Naira. He promised to help me with the money, but eventually, he would not keep his word."

"What type of project?"

"Dry season farming."

"Will you reconsider your new way of life if I help you with the money, as a gift, not a loan?" Kanem asked politely.

"I am no longer interested in the project. If I don't teach my uncle a lesson he will never forget, he will repeat it to another person in the future!" Dimba reacted furiously.

"There is a saying that 'two wrongs do not make a right.' Life is full of challenges. You may not understand why you are facing some challenges now, but if you hold on to what is right; you will one day understand."

Dimba listened carefully.

"It took me some years to understand that. I was angry with my people because of the way they maltreated me. Because of my bitterness and nasty way of life, I was banished from the village. On my way to Lagos to look for a job, I met a man in the bus who helped me understand life better."

Dimba was still listening.

"I am what I am today by the grace of God."

"You are the past, I am the present. I have already made up my mind on what to do to solve the problem!"

"God did not allow your uncle to help you because He has another way for you. I encourage you to calm down. Don't destroy yourself in your efforts to harm your uncle. Your future is not in the hands of your uncle. Closed doors don't remain closed forever."

"You look successful. You will never understand what I am facing. The joy of your success has already wiped out the memory of your past nasty experiences."

Kanem looked at Dimba calmly.

"Mine is fresh!"

"There are five ways of solving our problems: Good, better, best, bad and worse. Each has its result. I am only suggesting the best way for you, my friend. Right decisions are often painful, but those who use the opportunity end up in peace, not in pieces.

"I want to go and meet my friends!"

"Thank you for your time. My mentor once told me that 'a dry leaf under a tree is a warning to the green ones.'"

"What do you mean?" Dimba asked, as he stood up.

Kanem also stood up. "Others have acted worse than you are planning to act. Eventually, they harvested regret. It is good you learn from them. If I can become better, then there is hope for everyone. You are a potential leader. Now that many people are frustrated in your village, they need to see someone standing right, so that they can have hope for change. You are that right person; destroying your good potential means destroying the opportunities of helping your people to discover their potential."

"Thank you for your visit!"

"I hope you will not mind if I visit you again?"

Dimba moved away without saying a word.

Kanem stood in silence looking at him in pity and praying that God would help him realize his errors.

^

Nachau, Calvin and Kanem went out for a stroll on the outskirts of the village. On their way back, they met Ganduro. He was sitting alone on a rock looking at the river, as he worried over some challenges of life. Calvin introduced Nachau to Ganduro because he had already met Kanem. Nachau cheerfully greeted Ganduro, but Ganduro was reluctant in his response.

"How is your wife?" Calvin asked.

"With all due respect, I no longer have a wife."

"You are only going through tough times; but by God's grace, they will be over one day," Calvin assured.

"Marriage is not my priority now. I have other things to worry about!" Ganduro reacted in anger.

Nachau and Kanem listened, as they watched Calvin and Ganduro.

Calvin looked at Nachau. His facial expression showed an invitation to Nachau to contribute.

There was silence for awhile.

"It is a huge challenge to have tasted more of the bitter side of marriage, but that does not mean it is not good," Nachau said.

"I hate it because of my wife's attitude," Ganduro replied.

"There is a proverb that 'peace is achieved in marriage when there is a fool in it,'" Nachau mentioned.

"What do you mean, sir?" Ganduro quickly asked.

"'One of you has to be patient and this can appear foolish at first. If one is patient today, the other should return the gesture next time,'" Nachau explained.

"Only cowards become patient in life. There are many young girls in this village, who desperately desire marriage. I will choose one of them when I am ready to marry," Ganduro stated.

"Courage is seasonal. Every one of us is a coward once in awhile, which makes us qualified to choose patience," Nachau explained.

Ganduro listened carefully.

"Divorce is not the will of God for us. Every family has its problems. How you handle these problems is what makes the difference. How sure are you that the woman you will marry next will not be worse than the wife you accused of making life bitter for you? Divorce comes with bitter consequences," Nachau explained.

"What are they?" Ganduro curiously asked.

Nachau noticed that Kanem wanted to contribute to the discussion. "Do you have something to say on that note?"

"Yes, sir, "Kanem replied.

"Please, go ahead," Nachau encouraged.

"Divorce affects you spiritually, psychologically, socially, financially and in other aspects. It makes you unstable for future challenges. It also affects your leadership potential. If you cannot lead one woman, how can you lead your village when in the future the opportunity comes your way?" Kanem emphasized.

Nachau was very happy as he looked at Kanem explaining the realities of marriage to Ganduro. Calvin also looked on with interest.

"It can also affect your view of women, which may determine the manner in which you treat them. You will easily conclude that all women are the same," Kanem remarked.

Ganduro listened.

"It is very important for you to forgive your wife. It is cheaper to make use of forgiveness than to divorce," Kanem explained.

Ganduro listened thoughtfully.

"In a situation like this, it is better you examine yourself also, not just your wife. When you are the first to change your life, it is easier to ask your wife to make changes also," Kanem emphasized.

"I am grateful for your encouragement," Ganduro said after a moment of silence.

"We wish you well. Don't forget that nothing is impossible with God," Calvin commented.

CHAPTER 10

Eremale sent for Dimba to meet him in the house. When Dimba got the message, he thought long and hard wondering whether or not to go. Reluctantly, he eventually went. On getting to the house, he sat in the parlour and waited for his uncle for about two hours.

When Eremale came out, he welcomed Dimba and asked him to follow him outside. Dimba stood up slowly and followed his uncle. When they went out, Eremale showed him a place in his compound and asked him to help him cut the grass. Dimba suddenly became furious with his uncle. His face reflected the condition of his mind.

"I will be glad if you can help me today. I also want to remind you that I have not forgotten our last discussion."

Dimba still kept quiet looking at his uncle.

"How is your father's health?"

Dimba quietly moved away, trying to get out of the compound.

"Where are you going? You can't just walk out on me without saying a word! Do you realise just how disrespectful that is?"

Dimba stood in silence for a moment. He turned and looked at his uncle.

"Come here!" Eremale commanded.

Dimba slowly moved closer to his uncle.

"Will you do the job or not?"

"I am not your slave!" Dimba reacted bitterly.

"What did you say?" Eremale asked, surprisingly.

"I am sure you heard me well! You are the worst greedy man I have ever seen. Go and ask your wife and daughter to cut the grass for you!"

Eremale slapped Dimba. "Mind your words! I hope you have not forgotten that you are speaking to your uncle!"

Dimba slapped Eremale back, and then punched him on the nose. Eremale fell down on the ground with blood gushing out of his nose.

"I will kill you if you dare raise your hand against me again! I am not the Dimba you used to know!"

Eremale lay helplessly on the ground looking at Dimba.

Mem was attracted by the noise outside. She ran out and saw her husband on the ground. "What is going on here?" she asked, as she reached out to her husband.

"You will be sorry for what you just did!" Eremale threatened.

"This is the beginning of a battle between us! I will show you the bitterness of the monster you created. You can report me to anywhere you want to, but be warned that nobody can stop me from doing what I want to do!" Dimba responded.

"Dimba, are you mad? What has gone wrong with you?" Mem asked, deeply disturbed, as she helped her husband stand on his feet.

"You are the mad people here! You will receive your share if you talk to me like that again. You are also part of the evil. I will prove to you that greed does not lead to happiness. Those who think of their immediate family members alone don't deserve to live in our community!" Dimba reacted bravely while walking out of the compound.

"This boy is not in his right senses," Eremale wondered aloud, after Dimba had left the compound.

"What happened?"

"He was angry because I asked him to help me cut the grass. I lost my temper and slapped him. He retaliated because of that. I am sure he was angry with me for not assisting him."

"I think you are right that he was angry because you did not help him. We have to discipline him for his attitude, or else other people will disrespect you if they hear of what has happened," Mem advised.

"That is the best thing to do."

 "No matter what happens, he will not receive any help from us!" Mem stressed.

Eremale went into the house and dressed up. He quickly went and reported the matter to Dimba's father. Ntedu begged him to allow the family to handle the case; but Eremale refused. He reported the matter to the security station. Dimba was arrested and jailed.

Nachau, Calvin and Kanem heard of what happened. They knew that something urgent needed to be done to resolve the problem. Kanem quickly volunteered to go to the security station with Dimba's father to bail him out.

Ntedu did not hesitate to welcome Kanem's proposal when he shared it with him in his house. He was in tears when he went to the security station with Kanem, Tani, Omem and Ganduro. Ntedu walked slowly with much difficulty, using a staff. On reaching the security station, it took a lot of effort before Dimba was released on bail. Dimba was given a strong warning against a reckless lifestyle.

When they returned home, Dimba and his friends spoke in anger against Eremale's attitude. Ntedu sat silently thinking over the situation.

"It is possible to forgive your uncle," Kanem encouraged, moving closer to Dimba.

"Forgiveness is not in my plans!" Dimba shouted. "I will be a big fool if I forgive my uncle!"

Ntedu looked keenly at his son without uttering a word. His mood showed he was in support of what he was saying.

"Don't let your uncle's nature change yours. You should help in securing the future of your clan," Kanem advised.

"The clan is not important to me! My uncle will never stop regretting what he did!" Dimba responded.

Dimba's friends listened to the discussions with interest.

"There is a good future awaiting you. Don't reach it with injuries you can avoid. You will get good results if you are willing to put aside today's negative decision for tomorrow's comfort. There is always a better way of doing things. Helpful ideas often come after careful consideration," Kanem said.

Dimba stared at Kanem in anger.

"Don't fight a battle you can avoid. Jesus, the Saviour of the world loves you. He invites all those who are carrying heavy loads to come to Him and have rest," Kanem explained.

"No, rest is for the weak and lazy. I am strong! I can carry my burden by myself. I don't need the help of the Jesus you talk about. Thank you for your efforts. I need to go to somewhere now," Dimba stated. "Let us go," he said to his friends.

"You were not created to live for yourself. You can't make it on your own. Fighting your uncle will only magnify the evil that you can overcome through forgiveness. Build your future on the Rock, not on the sand. A storm is coming," Kanem warned.

Dimba and his friends went out of the compound.

"You need to talk to your son, sir," Kanem said to Ntedu.

"Let him go ahead and do whatever he wants to do. I am in support of him."

Kanem, on hearing that, was immediately aware that a major crisis was developing in the village. Any father who would support his son to do wrong was a strong sign of the death of hope. "You are supposed to be a good example to your son."

"I have nothing good in me to give him. His uncle deserves whatever has the name bad!" Ntedu furiously reacted.

"You can make your son a soft pillow for you in your old age. Whatever wrong he does now will affect you too."

"Thank you for your advice. I will think it over," Ntedu said reluctantly, just to avoid further discussion with Kanem.

"I wish you well," Kanem stated.

Dimba and friends went to their usual place to smoke marijuana. As they aggressively smoked, they discussed their plans for dealing with Eremale. The way Dimba smoked surprised his friends; it was as if he had been doing it for a long time.

^

When Kanem returned to Calvin's house, he met Nachau and Calvin sitting on stools under a tree outside the compound. Kanem greeted them and then went into the compound to fetch a stool to sit on. He sadly informed them of what had happened, emphasising Dimba's state of mind.

"Don't worry, your time of breakthrough will one day come. Building a foundation of anything is not easy," Nachau encouraged.

"I sense big trouble ahead. Dimba has never behaved the way he does now," Calvin said.

"Everybody has good and bad days. What matters is how a person handles himself and others. A good heart can be a stranger to good deeds if mismanaged," Nachau explained.

"He was as wild as a 'wounded lion.' I just hope he will not murder his uncle. From experience, I know what frustration can cause," Kanem commented.

"Storms don't last forever. Dimba will eventually realize that," Nachau stated.

"I hope it will not be too late for him," Calvin remarked.

"We must not give up on him. At the right time, God will give us success," Nachau said.

"How do we handle him better?" Kanem asked.

"Continue to depend on the Holy Spirit to convict him of sin. Focus on sowing helpful words into his heart. One day, these words will find ways to germinate. Don't forget that our hearts have blood in them. That means they are alive and they can respond to information," Nachau explained.

"Frustration is not a good manager. It should not be allowed to manage anybody," Kanem said in concern.

"That is the right spirit. The comfort we receive from our experiences becomes bigger when we share with others in need," Nachau commented.

"I wish you the best in handling Dimba. I will focus on his friends. I really feel strongly for them, especially Ganduro," Calvin remarked.

"Let us not forget that a soldier knows he can be hit by a bullet on a battlefield, yet he still proceeds to battle. Our task here is a battle against the kingdom of darkness. The evil one will use different ways to knock us down. We should always trust God for victory, and never be discouraged. Only strong people can help the weak," Nachau emphasized.

CHAPTER 11

The problem between Ganduro and Yalami remained unresolved. Both of them were finding life very difficult. Ganduro's mother insisted he must be reconciled with his wife. The family sent a message to Yalami's parents about their intended visit for reconciliation. When Amsami received the message, he called Malena and Yalami for a discussion.

"I have received a message from your husband's parents about their intention to visit us for a discussion," Amsami informed Yalami.

Yalami kept quiet.

"If this meeting is going to be successful, you need to be mentally prepared to be reconciled before they arrive."

"My daughter will not be reconciled with anybody unless I have concrete evidence that she will not suffer again in her husband's house!" Malena stated.

Amsami looked disrespectfully at his wife. "You are in your husband's house, but you don't want your daughter to be in her own house. That's selfish!"

"You can say whatever you want. I do not want my daughter to suffer again!"

"When are they coming?" Yalami asked calmly.

"On Monday, next week," Amsami replied.

"I will get prepared."

"I hope you are not trying to consider reconciling with your husband?" Malena inquired anxiously.

"I am getting tired of living here. I hate the way people gossip about me. Some of the girls at the stream abused me the last time I went to fetch some water," Yalami explained.

"Shut your mouth! What do you know about life? You will never be reconciled with your husband until I allow you!" Malena shouted.

"But Mummy, I will not stay with you forever."

"I am happy you are thinking of being reconciled to your husband. That is a good decision," Amsami emphasized.

"I will make life miserable for your in-laws when they come, so that you will not be reconciled with them. I am surprised at your acceptance of your father's advice, seeing he is responsible for our poverty. A woman should listen to a woman if she wants to be happy," Malena stressed harshly.

"Don't do that if you want peace in this house!" Amsami warned.

"There will be a serious crisis in this house if you try to stop me!" Malena responded angrily.

"Mummy, stop talking like that, please," Yalami said.

"Do you want to end up like me? I made a big mistake in marrying your father. Haven't you seen how we have suffered in this house because of poverty?"

Amsami looked at his wife in bitterness.

"I ended up in this house because I listened to my father, who advised me to marry your father. That is why I don't want you to listen to your father, because fathers don't understand much about feelings."

Yalami gazed at her mother in silence.

"I had warned you against marrying a poor man when you wanted to marry Ganduro, but you and your father persisted. What have you achieved from the marriage? Only misery."

Amsami and Yalami stared at Malena in concern.

"As a loving mother, I advise you to remain here for some time. I am sure a rich man will see you someday and marry you so that our family can be delivered from the frustration your father has brought upon us."

"You have no shame, Malena! You are the most senseless woman I have ever seen!" Amsami reacted.

"You are the most senseless man I have ever met!"Malena responded.

"If you ever say that to me again, I will make sure you regret it!"

Malena stood up, furious with her husband. "Try it and see. You will walk in shame for the rest of your miserable life on earth after I finish dealing with you!"

As usual, Amsami stood up and walked out of the house to avoid further confrontation with his wife. Malena rained insults on him as he went out. Amsami did not utter another word. Their neighbours heard Malena's shouting and cautiously complained about her attitude towards her husband. None of them had the courage to meet her to calm her down.

Yalami went into her hut, leaving Malena alone. Malena called Yalami to come back and listen to her, but Yalami refused to obey.

Amsami went straight to a local beer centre, made his order and drank in anger, as he thought about his wife's attitude. The idea of divorce crossed his mind, but he did not accept it as a way out because he did not want to be a bad example of marriage to his children.

Yalami fell on her bed crying bitterly, thinking over her problems.

^

Namo came to Calvin's compound for a discussion. His approach to the compound had completely changed. His face showed respect for the ministry God had placed in Calvin's care. Entering the house, he saw Calvin and others eating their lunch. They were happy to see him. Calvin quickly offered him a seat and invited him to join them in their meal. Namo wanted to decline the offer, but changed his mind quickly, in order to demonstrate to his new friends that they were now together. He took a portion of the food and ate.

After eating, he asked to see Nachau outside. Nachau and Namo stood up and went out. They sat on a stone by the entrance of Calvin's house.

"I am glad you have responded positively to my request of having a discussion with you in spite of the unarranged nature of it."

"You are welcome. I am glad you are here. It means a lot to us."

"My life has been restless since the last time you and your friends came to me. The way you spoke that day was remarkable. Nobody has ever shown me the way of life and ministry the way you did."

Nachau listened attentively.

"The night after your visit, I had an urge to meet you so that you could be a mentor to me. I discovered that day that I could learn a lot from you."

Nachau still listened.

"My pride didn't allow me to come to you the next day. I struggled hard to avoid coming. I am here to learn from you so that I can be more fruitful in ministry."

"I am glad you came," Nachau responded calmly after being silent for a moment.

"Thank you, sir."

"Our meeting with you did not take God by surprise. He arranged the moment and the right time for everything. It is not because I am better than Calvin, who has been speaking to you before now. I am only used by God to conclude what He has started through Calvin."

Namo nodded in understanding.

"After our discussions that day, I also had a strong conviction to contribute in diverse ways to your ministry. Your coming is further confirmation to me of that conviction. I am willing to be used by God to provide you with guidance in life and ministry. My task is to help people discover the purpose of life and how to achieve it for reconciliation to God."

Namo listened carefully.

"What is the mission of your ministry?"

"To reach lost people for the kingdom of God," Namo replied.

"That is good, but what do you mean by the kingdom of God?"

"It means to prepare people so that they can eventually be in heaven."

"It is good to focus first on helping them have a good relationship with Jesus before thinking of heaven, so that they will still be valuable on earth as they anticipate being with Jesus in heaven."

Namo listened.

"What is the major problem you are facing in ministry?" Nachau asked.

"The issue of growth. For some years, we have been toiling here, but the people have hardened their hearts to the gospel. We have given our best efforts, but only reap frustration."

"The problem may be exactly that you have been using your own best efforts; that may not be God's way of doing what He has called you to do. Someone says that 'when the devil cannot stop you from doing something for God, he will help you to do many things for God, so that in the end you do nothing for God.'"

"That is true."

"You need to know that your job is not to produce results, but to be used as an instrument to tell the good news. The Holy Spirit is responsible for convicting people of sin and moving them to repentance."

"Are you saying that I should not expect results in what I do?"

"You should expect results as you do the work, but don't focus on when and how the results will come. Just trust God to give you results in His own way and time."

Namo was quiet in deep reflection.

Nachau waited for him to talk.

"I am here by faith, trusting God to provide my needs; but I must confess that ministry has been tough without sufficient resources. Sometimes I tend to think that God has forgotten about us."

"If you come to me and inform me that you will be travelling to the city to visit someone, I will wish you a safe journey. However, when I am the one sending you to the city, it is my responsibility to provide the fare for your trip, feeding and accommodation, because the task is mine. If I don't sponsor the trip, that means the task will not be accomplished for me."

Namo listened.

"In the same way, God will never send you for His task, without sponsoring it. If you face some difficulties in the process, it is because He wants to help you grow to maturity," Nachau encouraged.

"You have really encouraged me to move on."

"To God be the glory."

"I believe God has brought you and your friends here for His purpose. I am sorry for my earlier attitude. Please, help me convey my apology to your colleagues, especially Calvin."

Nachau smiled. "Any time God seems not to make sense to you, just hold on, because the sense is in the making," he said.

"Thank you once again," Namo stated.

CHAPTER 12

Lah, full of curiosity, called Nachau to discuss his problems further. He did not have the usual network trouble in reaching Nachau this time around.

"Hello."

"Good afternoon, sir" Lah said.

"Good afternoon."

"How is the work moving?"

"We are trusting God for good results. How is your family?"

"Everybody is making progress. Thank you for your concern."

"What do we talk about today?"

"I want to hear your opinion on how to prevent or handle strikes by workers. There have been many strikes in my company. I tried different ways to handle them, but so far without success," Lah explained.

"What method have you been using?"

"The major one is threatening them with losing their jobs."

"That method usually leads to more strikes," Nachau commented.

Lah listened.

"What do the workers want from the company?"

"Most of their demands are centred on increased salaries."

Nachau kept quiet for a moment.

Lah waited anxiously.

"You need to know that there is often one major reason for workers to go on strike. Underneath it, there are other reasons."

Lah listened carefully with a pen in his hand and a jotter on the table in front of him.

"People who depend on their jobs as major means of survival go on strike because without the jobs, their lives are empty and full of frustrations. They fight for their salaries to be increased because that is the only way their lives can get better."

Lah started writing down some ideas.

"Some go on strike because they have personal business somewhere, which absence from work will enable them to develop further. Others do it because they hate their jobs. Someone says that 'people who do what they were created to do can afford to do that for free and still be happy.'"

Lah was still writing.

"The last group consists of people who focus on improving the system not only for their survival, but also to make the future better for others."

Lah smiled. "Thank you for opening up my mind," he said.

"To God be the glory."

"What can I do?"

"You will negotiate well with your striking workers when you understand their different reasons."

"Okay."

"You should also understand that it is less expensive to solve your workers' problems outside strike action than through it. No matter how long a strike action lasts, it will one day be resolved. Hence, preventing strikes is better than managing them, because many things are lost in its management. Innocent people suffer; there is a crippling of essential services, and an increase of bitterness and disrespect in the company. Successful strikes also encourage your staff to embark on more strikes in the future."

"I am already facing these challenges," Lah admitted.

"Bad or misunderstood decisions are often behind strikes. As a leader, you must double check your decisions before implementing them wisely."

"What about where the workers force a company's management into making unrealistic commitments, just because of restoring peace?"

Nachau smiled. "In most cases, the demands are only high, not unrealistic. High demands come because of insufficient information. When your workers think the company has unlimited resources, it is easy to ask for more."

Lah listened thoughtfully.

"In addition, management's expensive lifestyles also lead to high demands by the junior staff. They will not believe you when you tell them there is no money in the company to solve their problems when at the same time you buy expensive clothes, cars and build personal houses that cost more than they demand."

Lah nodded.

"It is important for you to always remember that wise leaders prevent strike actions or resolve them in just a few hours. Those leaders who ignore strikes don't understand life. Whatever positive steps you take to help in making today better may serve you well tomorrow."

Lah listened keenly.

"Your workers are not your tools, they are your partners. It is like the body, which is a unit. When the hand is on strike because of illness, the head and other parts of the body also feel the pain. If the hand is ignored, eventually, the rest of the body will be affected. Learn to love your staff more than yourself, and you will better understand the joy of leadership."

"I can now see clearly how I have been missing the mark of leadership."

"You must do whatever you can do to become a better leader. Good leadership is far more rewarding than bad."

Lah wrote some points.

"We are like oil in the engine of a car. We get burnt out when our mission on earth is over. Beauty cannot be seen and appreciated in the darkness. Light is necessary for all you do."

"Whenever I discuss with you, I feel like I have no understanding of life at all. You are really a gift to us in this nation and globally."

Nachau smiled. "Jesus is the only gift to this nation and the world that the Father has given to us for our salvation. I am only a tool in His hands."

Lah was quiet for a short time. "Thank you for your time. Once again, I am grateful. I wish you success in your mission," he said.

"Thank you. I wish you the same."

^

The day for the reconciliation meeting between Ganduro and Yalami had finally arrived. Amsami's house was full of guests from both villages. The meeting attracted many people because they wanted to maintain the unity between the two villages. Yalami's insults to the people of Romen were also on the agenda.

Ganduro, his people and friends sat on mats opposite Yalami and her parents. Silence ruled for awhile, as the two families looked at each other thoughtfully. Ganduro was pre-occupied with thoughts of his wife's earlier misbehaviour, wondering whether she had changed or not. Yalami too was thinking deeply about her husband's way of life. They kept on staring at each other without saying a word.

Hope of reconciliation was building high when Amsami broke the moment of silence by welcoming his guests to his compound and then commenced the meeting. Many discussions were held on the relationships between the two villages, and the problems between Ganduro and Yalami.

Yalami eventually apologized to the people of Romen for her insults. She passionately let them know how sorry she was, and her desire to be reconciled with her husband. Her apology was warmly welcomed.

Ganduro stood up peacefully with his head bowed in shame, and moved towards Malena, who was seated and staring at him angrily. When he got to her, he knelt down before her.

Malena furiously looked at Ganduro and his people. Everybody was in deep expectation of the outcome. Amsami hoped that Malena would not embarrass him or their guests as she had threatened earlier.

"I am sorry for the grief I have made you experience by abusing you. It was a mistake. It will never happen again!" Ganduro stated.

Suddenly, Malena gave Ganduro a slap on his cheek. "Go and ask your mother for forgiveness!"

Most of the people were surprised. Ganduro held his cheek, and looked at Malena speechlessly for a moment. Many people started talking against her action.

"Malena, stop that!" Amsami commanded.

Malena stood up in anger, getting ready for her next action.

"I still want to ask for your forgiveness," Ganduro insisted politely as he stood up.

Ganduro's friends saw the situation as a stain on their pride. They had expected him to walk away. They were disappointed by Ganduro's response to the insult.

Malena gave Ganduro another slap. "You and all the people in your village are idiots! My daughter is not going back to people who are lazy and good for nothing!"

Ganduro turned and looked at his friends who were still battling with anger. The elders in the meeting were all worried. Amsami once again commanded his wife to shut up and sit down; but she remained disobedient. Yalami could not control her emotions. She started crying.

Ganduro furiously pushed Malena down. She fell on her back and started shouting, calling on people to see what Ganduro had done. The meeting became noisy. Yalami's elder brother, Kunteri, rushed to Ganduro and punched his face. Ganduro fell down bleeding from his nose. Dimba ran to the scene and retaliated against Kunteri. Suddenly, the place was in confusion. It was beyond the control of the elders. The young people at the meeting venue fought each other wildly. Dimba was at the forefront of the fight. His strength was without equal. He singlehandedly injured Kunteri and two other young people.

It took a quick intervention of the security agents from the local station in the village to calm the crisis. The people of Romen narrowly escaped to their village. Dimba and his friends threatened further reprisals.

The security agents tried to make some arrests, but the elders from the two villages pleaded with them to allow them to handle the matter.

Many people blamed Malena for her wickedness. Yalami yelled at her mother and called her a wicked woman, who was not helping anybody. Amsami made no attempt to stop Yalami from insulting her mother.

Malena was speechless, as she listened to Yalami's insults. Kunteri and two other young men who were injured were rushed to the village clinic for treatment. Tension increased among the people in both villages.

Dimba and his friends were later summoned by the Village Head of Romen to try to persuade them to apologize to Kiringa people for their attitude; but they refused to do so. Under Dimba's leadership, they stood up and walked out of the Village Head's palace.

The Village Head and his elders could not believe what they saw. The thing that got their attention most was Dimba's attitude. They wondered what could have caused his strange behaviour. The Village Head sent the palace guards after them, but they all escaped into the jungle not far from the village, threatening to kill the guards if they made a further attempt to arrest them. The guards were afraid of the threats and gave up the chase.

Meanwhile, a similar tension was rising in Kiringa. The Village Head summoned the young people under Kunteri's leadership. They were warned against taking the law into their own hands, because there was a rumour going around about them attacking the Romen youth.

^

News of the crisis reached Nachau, Kanem and Calvin. "We need to move fast to stop this crisis becoming more serious," Nachau commented.

"We should follow Dimba and his friends into the jungle. They need us now before it is too late," Kanem said passionately.

"It is our mission to reach them with the message of hope. However, right now they will be aggressive towards anyone who approaches them, because they have been injured," Nachau stated.

Eventually, they went into the jungle. The moment Dimba and his friends spotted them from afar, they shouted a warning to them to back off or regret their actions.

Nachau and his friends introduced themselves and walked slowly towards them, as they explained their reason for the visit.

"We come in peace to talk with you," Nachau said.

"We don't want you to come closer!" Dimba responded angrily.

"We are not in the mood to see anyone!" Tani reacted.

"We really want to see you. We bring hope and peace," Nachau stated.

Suddenly, there was silence. Dimba and his friends were hit hard by Nachau's words.

"You can come over," Dimba said.

Nachau and his friends went to them. They all sat under a tree.

"What do you have to say to us?" Omem asked.

Nachau pointed to Calvin and Kanem to speak.

"Life has no meaning without living for something worthwhile. I am sure you now think that nobody cares for you," Calvin remarked.

"We don't think, we know! We would not be away from the village if people cared for us!" Dimba replied angrily.

"Something is wrong, that is why you are here. When you discover whatever is wrong and solve it, you will be able to break down the walls of fear and bitterness that surround you," Calvin explained.

"We could organize ourselves here to deal with the people who make life miserable for us," Dimba stated.

"A proverb says, 'any woman who sells eggs in the market does not start a fight.' When you focus on what you will lose by fighting, instead of what you will gain, you will have a strong motivation for dialogue and reconciliation between your people and the Kiringa people," Kanem contributed.

"It is never too late to make things right, my friends," Calvin encouraged.

Dimba and his friends listened thoughtfully.

"No one is useless. God will not create and sustain a useless person," Nachau said.

Dimba and his friends still listened.

"Building hope requires hopeful builders. There are different roads in this world. Some begin smoothly and end up roughly, while others start roughly and end up smoothly. The choice of which road to use is ours to make," Nachau remarked.

"We have already made our choices. The Kiringa youth have added to the insults we have been battling. They have tested us and discovered what we can do. However, they did not know all that we can do. They will never have peace in that village again. We are going to them as lions attacking their prey! No one can stop us from achieving our aim!" Dimba vowed.

"Yes!" the other friends supported.

"Crisis is like a telescope, it brings reasons for fighting closer even when they are far away. Only through love can we overcome people that are against us," Nachau responded

Dimba and friends were quiet for a short time.

"Life is boring without people who give us tough times," Kanem stated. "We always need to work hard to at least prove some people wrong. Tough times of life are like a night journey; no matter how long it lasts, gradually, bright morning eventually shows itself. Jesus is willing to give you peace if all of you will trust in Him," he emphasized.

"We are done with you. Please, leave us alone to think and plan!" Dimba reacted.

Nachau, together with his friends, continued to persuade Dimba and his friends to change their minds, but they refused. They warned Nachau and his friends not to inform security agents of their hide-out. They planned to keep on changing their hiding places.

Eventually, Nachau and his friends went back to the village, thinking further about new ways of reaching them.

CHAPTER 13

Next day, early in the morning, Nachau was speaking on the phone with his wife when calls kept on coming in. Despite that, he refused to end his discussions with her. He was informed that his son, Mijah, was ill. Ndatam, his daughter, had gone to school at the time of the call.

"I will be on my way today by God's grace," Nachau said.

"There is no need. I can take care of the situation by the grace of God. The work you do over there is equally important. You don't have to leave it. They need you now more than before," Akio urged.

"I understand your point; but the family is also a mission field. I have a responsibility to care for my family," Nachau explained.

"Thank you for your consideration. That is why I love you so much. I will prepare your favourite dish."

Nachau smiled. "I can never stop loving you."

"We would be happy to see you home. Mijah will be stronger with you around. You know he is just like you."

"Tell him to trust Jesus for his healing. You should also remind him of his favourite proverb."

"'No matter how short a person is, his eyes can see the sky,'" Akio quickly said.

"That is good."

"He said it to me twice today."

"Is he close by?"

"He is in his room."

"Let me speak with him."

"Okay," Akio said, while walking to Mijah's room to give him the cell phone.

"Hello, Daddy," Mijah said faintly, after receiving the cell phone.

"Hello, my son. How are you feeling?"

"I am looking up to see the sky."

Nachau smiled. "Keep on looking. Jesus will not let you down. He is in control of your situation. Let His strength be your strength," Nachau encouraged.

"It is just a trial. I know it will pass. I am a soldier of Jesus. Soldiers of Jesus are not afraid of circumstances around them."

Nachau smiled.

"Daddy?"

"Yes."

"Mummy told me that your work over there is becoming very difficult."

"Yes."

"You should always look up to the Lord. He will never abandon you. You are more than a conqueror. I am proud of you."

Nachau's eyes were full of tears of joy as he listened to his son.

"I remember what you once told me, that those who can dance in the midst of trials are indeed courageous. You also told me that fear fears faith."

"Thank you, my son, for your timely encouragement."

"To God be the glory," Mijah replied.

Nachau smiled. "I am also proud of you."

Mijah also smiled. "Greet your co-workers."

"I will," Nachau remarked.

Mijah gave the cell phone to his mother.

"Mijah has really encouraged me."

"I told you that your son is just like you," Akio stressed with a smile.

"I thank God for His blessings to us."

"I agree with you."

"Till I come. I love you."

"I love you more," Akio said teasingly.

Nachau was very happy. When he checked his cell phone after the conversations, he saw five missed calls. All came from Lah. Quickly, he called back. Lah picked the phone without wasting time, and asked to call Nachau back.

"The secret of progress is not to always be on the receiving side. It is good to also give what you have, no matter how small," Nachau explained.

"I have sufficient units in my cell phone. I don't want you to waste yours over my problems."

"There is a teaching that 'more is given to those who have.' The rain doesn't avoid blessing the ocean simply because the ocean has much water."

Lah smiled. "I surrender, sir."

"What do we talk about today?"

"I am very interested in employing youth, to ensure that nobody is idle among them. I have tried some things to bring youth on board, but I have not succeeded much. Many of them still get involved in drugs and drinking alcohol, while some are into armed robbery. The fact is that my company cannot employ them all. I am worried."

Nachau listened eagerly.

"My fear is that if we don't engage the youth today, we will regret it tomorrow."

Nachau, as often, kept quiet thinking.

Lah waited anxiously.

"The next principle is that direct and indirect methods of employment are both good."

"What does that mean?"

"The direct method is the one you use to employ the youth as staff in your company. The indirect is the one where you help them discover and become better in their various areas of potential, so that on their own, they can also employ others to work for them," Nachau explained.

Lah listened very carefully.

"Most companies employ people only to strengthen labour for much productivity in service. This idea is good, but it is also effective to employ people so that the people can become better."

"Won't that add much pressure to the budget of the company?"

"You have to compare and contrast the money you will spend on repairing the damage people can cause to your company if they are neglected, with the amount you will spend in making them better. With the right motive and vision, you can easily achieve good results."

"I understand."

"If you consider your ways carefully, I am sure that the amount you spend on your family alone in a month, as a company owner, can take care of the salaries of at least five junior workers."

"I agree with you," Lah admitted quickly.

"You must learn to develop today for the good of tomorrow."

"You have readymade answers to questions."

"To God be the glory. Good answers are always possible; but it takes courage to say them."

Lah smiled. "How do I achieve the indirect method?"

"Everyone has potential. Some cannot fit into direct employment. Locate them and support them to grow in their various businesses. Make sure they understand the need to build others too as they grow."

"Should these people be extensions of my company?"

"That is not the point. Let them own their companies. Yours is only to support them."

"How can I avoid abuse of my help by those that I support?"

"You cannot avoid that completely. Be ready to suffer some disappointments; but certainly, some of them will make the best use of their opportunities. The joy of the few successful ones will overshadow the bitterness of those that will mismanage their opportunities."

"I hope I can withstand the pressure of those that will fail," Lah remarked.

"There is great strength in facing anticipated problems. Let your positive eyes find good in every negative thing you see."

"I will do just that. Thank you, sir, for everything."

"One more thing."

Lah listened.

"I will also advise you to diversify your business to avoid full dependence on oil. Agriculture is a good option."

"Okay."

"You should think carefully about it. When you accept its potential, you can try investing in Romen. There is great agricultural potential there. When utilized well, the result will be great. Many people will also have job opportunities."

"I am glad you mentioned it. I have also been thinking about diversification in business. Your advice came at the right time."

"It is important you think about it well."

"I will certainly give it much consideration," Lah remarked.

After the discussions, Nachau prepared and drove home, using Kanem's car. The journey was successful. His time with the family was great. Mijah felt stronger when he saw his father just as Akio had predicted. Ndatam, their daughter, was also happy to see her father. The next day in the afternoon, Nachau drove back to Romen.

CHAPTER 14

Eremale and Mem were asleep when their two dogs began to bark loudly. The security man who worked in the house was not controlling the situation. Eremale woke up from sleep and peeped through the window. He couldn't get a clear view of what was going on in the darkness outside because of power failure.

Eremale called his dogs' names to try and silence them, but they were still uncontrollable. He shouted the name of the security man several times, but there was silence.

Eremale and Mem were worried over the situation. He picked his searchlight and went to the door. Suddenly, he heard the two dogs making a strange noise and then silence followed. Mem, who was shaking with fear behind her husband, urged him not to open the door.

Eventually, Eremale summoned his courage and opened the door. Immediately, he saw four men dressed in black with covered faces, holding machetes and rushing out of hiding. The men shouted at them to lie down. Quickly, Eremale and Mem obeyed. "Don't kill us, please! We have enough money to give you!" Eremale said in fear.

One of the armed robbers kicked Eremale and shouted at him to keep quiet. He ordered him to go and bring the money. Fearfully, Eremale stood up. Two of the armed robbers escorted him to his bedroom for the money.

Angela, their daughter, came out of her room to the parlour, because she had been awakened by the noise. She too was ordered to lie down. Fearfully, Mem begged the armed robbers to spare their lives. Angela started crying on realizing what was happening.

One of the armed robbers commanded them to keep quiet. They quickly obeyed. Mem started praying silently for deliverance. Eremale, and the armed robbers who escorted him, came out with a bag, containing a huge sum of money, held by one of the armed robbers.

The armed robber who seemed to be their leader did not say a word. He only controlled the situation with his hand. Mem was also commanded by one of the armed robbers to go and bring her jewellery, which she did quickly. The armed robbers put the jewellery in the moneybag.

Suddenly, one of the armed robbers lifted a heavy stick he was holding and hit Eremale hard on his back three times. Eremale shouted in pain. His wife and daughter cried, as they begged them to spare their lives.

"You will never forget this day!" one of the armed robbers said in anger.

Eremale was still groaning in pain, when the armed robbers rushed out of the compound with their stolen items. Mem and Angela rushed to Eremale, shouting for help. Eremale tried to move his legs, but it was hard for him. His body was not responding well. Suddenly, the security man rushed to the scene.

"Where have you been?" Mem furiously shouted at him.

"Madam, they attacked me first and tied me up in my room," the security man replied nervously.

"There is no point in having you here! Look at what they have done, because of your carelessness!"

"Sorry madam. I tried my best."

"Shut up and help us!" Mem reacted, as they gave Eremale a helping hand. His pain became severe. Mem called some neighbours using cell phones. It took some time for two people to come to the compound. Most of their neighbours refused to come because of Eremale's bad attitude.

Eventually, Eremale was rushed to the hospital in the city. After a series of tests, it was discovered that Eremale's spinal cord had been badly affected. The chances of him being on his feet again were slim. The robbery was later reported at the security station.

The armed robbers, on reaching their den, unmasked themselves and hurriedly checked the money and jewellery. "My uncle deserved what he got," Dimba, who led the operation, said.

"We are now rich. Those who refused to help us grow will go down with us," Tani remarked, as he smiled over the money he had seen.

"My wife will not call me a lazy man again. This money should convince her that I have a bright future," Ganduro boasted.

"We are talking about money; you are talking about your useless wife. It is like you are not in your right senses," Tani said.

Ganduro smiled. "Nachau told us that nobody is useless, or have you forgotten that?"

The other friends laughed at him.

"We will use this money to fight the evil people in this community. The youth in this village will never be slaves to anybody again!" Dimba said.

The friends shared the loot and each of them had his plan of what to do with his share. Meanwhile, the security agents started investigating the case.

CHAPTER 15

Late at night, the moon was shining. The Village Head of Kiringa's compound was on fire. People shouted and tried to quench the fire. It took concerted efforts to extinguish the flames, after they had caused considerable damage to the palace. The Village Head immediately invited his elders for an emergency meeting. Tensions were very high because they suspected Romen people to be behind this, especially because of the bitterness and threats they had received earlier from some of the Romen young men.

As the elders were discussing the probable cause of the fire, the youth had already mobilized themselves to head for Romen. They sneaked into the village and set fire to two huts in the Village Head's compound. The palace guards were taken by surprise. After the operation, the youth quickly retreated to Kiringa. One of the Village Head's daughters, died because of the attack. She was trapped in one of the huts.

The news of what the Kiringa youth had done shocked their elders and made them very angry.

Meanwhile, tension in Romen was also escalating. The youth had mobilized themselves. Dimba and his friends used the opportunity to return to the village because some of the young men had earlier gone and informed them about what had happened.

The Village Head also supported the youths' desire for vengeance. Dimba immediately took the lead. He charged the youth not to be afraid, but to stand up in defence of their land and deal with Kiringa people. "Today, we have the opportunity to show how strong we are. Our response to what was done to us will show that we are lions not lambs! Romen is a village that cannot be defeated. We will show Kiringa that we are the greatest!"

"Yes!" the youth responded together. Many of them went into their rooms and came out with different weapons, mostly machetes, bows and arrows.

Nachau, Calvin and Kanem rushed to the scene. The situation they saw disturbed them. They tried to persuade the Village Head to restrain his youth from vengeance, but the Village Head would not say anything against the youths' intentions. He continued weeping over the death of his daughter. The weeping of the women in the compound was uncontrollable.

Kanem rushed to Dimba to talk sense into him. Dimba pushed him aside and Kanem fell down on the ground.

"I have a mission to change our village. Nobody can stop us from attacking Kiringa. Get out of our way if you still cherish your life!" Dimba warned.

Kanem looked up at him in silence and pity.

"My mind is already hardened!" Dimba shouted.

Kanem stood up, not minding the dust on his clothes. "I understand what a hardened mind is. God made mine soft. Today I am benefiting from that. You can still be better if you don't give up. Love is the most important weapon against your enemy. Violence leads to more violence," Kanem commented.

"Don't mention your God here. He doesn't care for us. We have passed through sufferings in this village. Nobody was willing to help us become better! There is no hope now or later!" Dimba shouted in anger.

"Don't let frustration enslave you!" Kanem urged.

"If frustration leads me to vengeance, then it is a good master," Dimba responded, as he walked away from Kanem to lead his friends.

Kanem looked at him with a worried expression on his face.

As the youth got ready to attack Kiringa, the elders of Kiringa did not allow the matter to linger. The noise they heard from Romen convinced them that all was not well. That night they rushed to Romen to dialogue with the Village Head and elders.

However, on sighting them, the young men of Romen chased them. They caught the weak ones among them and beat them up. As a result, some sustained injuries; but all narrowly escaped back to Kiringa.

That night, on their border, a battle began between the two villages. The young men fought each other mercilessly. A few of them died, while many sustained injuries. The local security agents could not handle the matter. They called for reinforcements from the city. Early in the morning, the presence of security agents was heavy in the two villages.

Some arrests were made, but Dimba and some of his friends had returned to the jungle to hide. Many people in both villages were weeping over the loss of their loved ones. A curfew was imposed, from

5pm to 6am with the order that the security agents should deal with anybody disrupting the peace in the villages.

^

The next night, Dimba sneaked into their family compound to see his father. On reaching there, he found his father already in bed, but the light in the room was on.

"Who is it?" Ntedu asked, immediately he heard a knock.

"It is me, Papa."

"Come in. The door is not locked. I have been expecting you," Ntedu said, while adjusting himself on the bed to welcome his son.

Dimba opened the door and entered. "How are you doing, Papa?"

"I am still struggling. I hope you are doing okay?"

"Not too good, but still strong," Dimba replied and sat on a stool beside his father.

"What is the development about the crisis?"

"We are making plans to attack them again."

"How do you hope to handle the security agents?"

Dimba laughed. "Have you forgotten that this is our territory? We know how to avoid them."

"Be very careful. The security agents are professionals."

"We will be careful, Papa."

"Check under my bed and you will see something."

"What is it?" Dimba asked anxiously.

"Just check and tell me what you see."

"I see a gun," Dimba said, when he was removing the gun from underneath the bed, wrapped in cloth.

"Do you know how to use it?"

"Not very well; but I am sure I can learn fast," Dimba stated, as he continued to admire the gun.

"It is very easy to learn."

"Teach me, Papa."

Ntedu took some time to demonstrate to Dimba how to use the gun. Dimba was happy to learn some tips from his father.

"Take the gun and use it to defend yourself and ensure that the struggle becomes successful," Ntedu said.

"I am grateful for the gift. It will be used well."

Ntedu removed some money from underneath his pillow and gave to Dimba. "Take this; no struggle is successful without money."

"Where did you get the money?" Dimba asked.

"Just take the money."

"We have some money."

"Where did you get it?" Ntedu quickly asked.

"It is a long story."

Ntedu kept quiet for a moment. "I still insist that you take this money as my contribution."

"Okay, Papa," Dimba said, as he took the money.

"I have a question to ask you, just for confirmation," Ntedu stated, after silence for awhile.

"What is it?"

"It was reported to me that Eremale was injured by some armed robbers. I was told that his condition is bad. Do you have any idea of those behind it?"

Dimba was silent.

"You shouldn't have injured him," Ntedu said, after interpreting Dimba's silence.

"I wanted to make him feel the pain of your condition. If he cannot walk, he will understand what it means for you to be in this condition!"

"You thought well, my son. Go now before it is too late."

"Thank you," Dimba remarked, as he stood up to go.

"Tomorrow in the afternoon, by 2pm, there will be a blue van at the market square. You should meet the driver and tell him that you are my son. He will give you a consignment. Someone will be there with him.

He will spend two days in the village to train you and other youth on how to use the contents of the package."

"What is in the package?"

"Don't be in a hurry. You will know it when you open it. Be careful with the items. Treat the contents as top secret.

"Okay," Dimba agreed, as he went out.

The next day, as his father had told him, he met the blue van at the exact place. He introduced himself and received the consignment. The man his father said would train them went with him to the jungle.

When they eventually opened the consignment, to the surprise of Dimba and his friends, they saw new guns and bullets. The man informed them that some people provided them so that they could protect themselves in any crisis with Kiringa. Dimba and his friends asked a series of questions during the training, to which the man provided the right answers. In two days, they were trained in how to use the guns.

CHAPTER 16

The Village Head buried his daughter in his compound, but the rest of the dead in both villages were respectively given mass burials.

After that, Kanem started the mobile clinic. Kiringa people also heard of Kanem's services, but fear stopped them coming. Kanem tried to reach them, but the walls of hatred between the two villages were still strong. He prayed that God would open up opportunities for him to use his profession to reconcile the villages.

Nachau and Calvin went to the Village Head of Romen for a discussion. The security agents spent some time checking people, especially motorists and motorcyclists. Nachau noticed that some check-ups were thorough, while others were not. Those who were able to give a handshake to some of the security agents with something in their hands passed easily. Those who refused, suffered delay and expressions of annoyance from some of the security agents. The key question the security agents asked the people, as Nachau noticed, was 'What do you have for us?' Nachau and Calvin were stopped and searched. The security agents searching smiled at them and asked the usual question in expectation of the usual token.

"The only thing we have for you is a piece of advice. You are an instrument of peace and stability; don't abuse the privilege. Your actions affect this place. Make people smile, not cry," Nachau said boldly.

"Go!" one of the security agents ordered them, after thinking over Nachau's advice for a moment.

Quietly, Nachau and Calvin moved away.

"Our security systems are corrupt. I wonder what kind of security they can offer," Calvin stated.

"Don't generalize. Some of them still do their job well. Corruption is not the problem of one section of the country. It has affected various sectors.

"You are right," Calvin admitted.

Finally, they reached the Village Head's house. They were lucky to meet him sitting outside his compound with his elders sitting on a mat before him. The presence of the security outfit was also evident at his compound.

"You are welcome," the Village Head said.

"Thank you, sir, "Nachau and Calvin replied respectively as they sat on the mat.

"What can I do for you?" the Village Head asked.

"We want to discuss with you the current developments between Kiringa and Romen," Calvin mentioned.

"The Village Head is not in the mood to discuss such things now," Nupam, one of the elders, remarked. He was tall and dark with much grey hair on his head. Many people in the village were of the opinion that he was the most influential person among the Romen elders.

Nachau and Calvin kept quiet in anticipation of a direct reply by the Village Head.

"You can discuss other things, but not the issue you mentioned," Nupam added.

"We are worried because of what is now happening. The current developments will soon affect us all, even worse than they do now, if we don't move fast to curtail the situation. A question was asked, 'When a fire disaster begins on the river, how do we stop it?'" Nachau asked.

There was silence for a moment. The Village Head and his elders looked at each other.

"As leaders, we are like the river. Let us not allow the disaster to derive its strength from us. It will be difficult to stop it," Nachau explained.

"This is not your village, it is better you allow the inhabitants to handle their problems the way they see fit," the Village Head said.

Nachau and Calvin were shocked by the words of the Village Head. "Once a river is polluted, many things are affected if nothing positive is done to stop it from spreading," Nachau clarified.

The Village Head and others stared at Nachau.

"Boundaries have separated us, but we are one. We have already become part of your people. I am sure you will not leave me in a well when I fall into it simply because I am not from this village," Nachau emphasized.

The Village Head was quiet for some time. "What advice do you have concerning the current developments?" he asked.

"Thank you for the opportunity to contribute. Based on my understanding, your village and Kiringa are the biggest in this Local Government Area. God has a reason for that. Your people, especially the youth, have gone wild. Weapons of war are in the hands of many people. Romen needs to be reconciled with Kiringa before more lives and possessions are lost," Nachau said.

"That will never happen! They attacked us first!" Nupam shouted.

"Please, let us pay attention to what he is saying," Puri, one of the elders, remarked calmly.

"Puri is right, let us pay attention," the Village Head agreed.

Nupam kept quiet, but his face still showed disapproval of reconciliation with Kiringa.

"We should help build a future that our children will enjoy. If we don't train our children to avoid violence today, they will soon get used to it as the best way of solving their problems. One day, when these crises are over, they will certainly use violence against us," Nachau explained.

"Are you suggesting that we fold our hands and watch the Kiringa people kill us? They attacked us first. I hope you have not forgotten that?" the Village Head asked gently.

"We must do whatever we can do to stop destruction from progressing. No matter how long the problems last, they must be settled one day. Why not now? It takes two people to fight. If we forgive them, that means reducing the strength of the crises, which will lead to reconciliation. Maturity is also seen in a person's ability to forgive."

The Village Head and others listened attentively.

"Someone said that 'blood attracts blood.' Bloodshed waters the seeds of hatred and vengeance for easy germination from one generation to another. Every wicked heart is tormented by guilt when it fights against love," Nachau explained further.

The Village Head nodded in understanding.

"There was a fire disaster in Kiringa before they attacked Romen. Judging from the disastrous outcome of the attempted reconciliation of Ganduro's marital conflicts with Yalami, I think they assumed Romen caused the fire. There is a saying that 'when a thorn injures a person's leg on a groundnut farm that is not his own, he should not bend down to remove the thorn,'" Nachau said.

"Why?" the Village Head inquired.

"The farm owner will think the person is trying to remove his groundnuts," Nachau answered.

Suddenly, there was silence again. The Village Head and the elders were deep in thought.

Calvin smiled in anticipation.

"You spoke with much wisdom. What is the secret behind it?" the Village Head asked.

"Jesus is the source of my strength. He teaches me to love my enemies and do good to those who make life miserable for me. In that way, they would be put to shame."

"Calvin has told me of Jesus. I will send for you another time to explain more. I will take some time to think over what you have said," the Village Head stated.

"Thank you once again for the opportunity to talk," Nachau remarked.

"I hope you are not thinking of reconciling with Kiringa, your highness? Don't allow these people to deceive us. They may be agents working for our enemies," Nupam warned, after the departure of Nachau and Calvin.

"I have never heard anyone speak like that man. I think he can help us at a time like this," the Village Head responded.

"I agree with you, your highness," Puri added.

CHAPTER 17

Yalami had refused to help her mother in any household work despite all the orders she had received from her. "You deceived me into staying here so that I will be your slave! Enough is enough! I will never work in this house again. This is your house; you need to manage it yourself!" Yalami protested.

"If you don't wash these dishes now, you will see a side of me that you have never seen!" Malena threatened.

"There is no side of you that I have never seen, Mama! All I know is that you are a wicked mother who stops her family's progress. You are the worst mother I have ever seen!"

Malena slapped Yalami hard. "I will curse you if you call me wicked again. All I sought to do was to protect you from suffering!"

Yalami held her cheek for awhile, as she frowned, looking directly at her mother. "If you slap me again, I will prove to you that it is normal for a tiger's cub to act as its mother!"

"You mean you will slap me back?"

Suddenly, Kunteri and Amsami walked into the compound.

Malena slapped Yalami again. "Do your worst, and let me see."

Yalami slapped her mother. "You have pushed me to the limit. I no longer have respect for you. This family will be better off without you! The blood of all the people who have been killed because of the crises will be on you!"

Amsami and Kunteri rushed to the scene. "Are you mad?" Kunteri asked Yalami angrily.

Yalami in anger stared at her mother and Kunteri.

Malena in surprise went quietly and sat on a stool, looking at her daughter and wondering how she got the courage to slap her. It suddenly dawned on her that she needed to be careful with Yalami.

Amsami just stood as a spectator. In his mind, he knew that what Yalami did was wrong, but it served his wife right, because the time for reaping had come. Part of him wished Yalami would do more, but he restrained the flow of negative thoughts about his wife.

"No wonder your husband sent you out of his house!" Kunteri said.

"If you don't want your share of my anger, I advise you to stay out of this or you will regret your life this moment!" Yalami warned.

"What can you do?"

Yalami held the collar of Kunteri's shirt. "Grow up and look for something good to do rather than hanging around your parents for survival. Many of your friends are married and working hard for a better life, but you are here without a focus. I pity your life!" Yalami responded.

"Papa, tell Yalami to let go of my shirt or I will slap her."

"Slap me if you think you are courageous!" Yalami yelled at him.

Amsami intervened and asked Yalami to go into her room. She went in reluctantly, still furious. Kunteri left the compound in anger. Malena was still sitting silently on the stool, pondering what to do to Yalami. Her attitude seemed to be beyond control. Amsami looked at his wife strangely and hissed, as he went into his room.

After some minutes, Yalami came out of the room with her bag, getting set to leave the compound for her husband's house. Amsami saw her from his room through the partly open door. He quickly went out to talk to her. Malena still would not say anything. She knew that any further word from her might lead to cursing Yalami.

"Where are you going?" Amsami asked.

Yalami did not talk. Tears rolled down her cheeks.

"I hope you are not leaving this house now?"

"I am leaving for my husband's house. I regret coming back to this place!"

"You cannot do that now. The tension between the two villages is still high. It is risky for you."

"Death is better than living in this house!"

"Don't forget that you grew up here. This moment will be over soon. I am not stopping you from returning to your husband, because that has been my desire and I am sure you know that."

"I know, Papa. Mama hates me. She does not want me to be happy. It is better I leave this house. I am willing to face the danger ahead!" Yalami persisted.

Malena still remained calm and quiet, contemplating the situation.

Yalami moved out of the compound with her bag. Some of the villagers who saw her walking towards Romen rushed to her father's house and inquired about what was wrong.

When she reached the stream before Romen, some Romen women saw her and quickly attacked her angrily. They beat her so hard that she sustained a deep cut on her forehead. Blood gushed out of the deep cut down her chest.

Yalami screamed for help, which attracted the security agents. It was hard for the security agents to rescue her from the angry women. The women were eventually arrested. Yalami was rushed to the local clinic, which was in Kiringa. Having seen Yalami's condition and being informed by her of what had happened, the Kiringa youth became angry and shouted "Enough is enough!"

Amsami and Malena, on receiving the news, forgot their differences and rushed to the clinic to see their daughter and support her.

^

The next morning, by 8am, the immediate situation had been brought under control. Both villages were calm.

Some women from Romen were busy washing in the stream at the spot where Yalami was attacked. Suddenly, Kunteri and some other youths from Kiringa broke the uneasy calm and attacked them. Most of them were injured. Kunteri and two others raped the youngest one among the women, by name Lamem. She was the daughter of the Village Head of Romen. She lost her virginity as a result.

As the women escaped to Romen with injuries and spread the story of the attack and rape, tension mounted high again. The security agents found it hard to calm the situation. They fired gunshots in the air to scare people away. Eventually, their tactics worked. Calmness was restored for a short time.

Kunteri and his friends denied any involvement in the attack and rape when they were summoned and questioned by security agents. Some of their elders supported them. Eventually, Kunteri and friends were released.

However, the Village Head of Romen was extremely bitter about the attack and rape of his daughter.

In order to help the two villages, Nachau and his friends came together and prayed to God for more effective ways of handling the situation.

The curfew was tightened, from 5pm to 12 noon. People were not happy with the development, because it affected the villages' economic and social life. Despite the increased security, people were anxious and ready for self-defence in case of any surprise attack.

At 12:30 am, the weather was cold; many people were in a deep sleep in Kiringa when Dimba and his friends attacked, shooting indiscriminately and setting houses on fire. Kunteri and a few people ran out of the village. Some people were killed, including women and children. Dimba and his friends exchanged fire with the security agents before they managed to escape. Omem was shot in the leg, but his friends were able to help him escape with them.

Weeping was heard all over Kiringa as black smoke rose, piercing through the darkness. Bitterness and sorrow ruled the village. The security agents tried to bring the situation under control.

Meanwhile, in their jungle hideout, Dimba and his friends were attending to Omem. Blood kept gushing out from the wound, as Omem cried loudly for relief. Ganduro, however, sat on a rock thinking about his wife and hoping she had not been hit by a stray bullet during the attack.

Dimba stood up and addressed his friends as he struggled to be strong. "We have caused much harm to our enemies. We must get ready to face the consequences of our actions. We must fight to the finish to protect our village from total destruction."

His gang listened attentively.

"No matter what happens, none of you should forget that we did not start this crisis. We were attacked by the people of Kiringa, and it is our duty to defend ourselves!" Dimba explained.

"What do we do about Omem?"Tani asked anxiously. "He is losing much blood."

Dimba kept quiet for a moment. "We cannot take him to the clinic. We will look after him here."

"He will die if we don't take him to the clinic," Tani emphasized.

"If we take him to the clinic, we will be handing ourselves over to the security agents," Dimba said.

"Help me!" Omem screamed.

Squatting down, Dimba calmly encouraged Omen. "We will solve the problem. Be strong, my friend."

Omem nodded as he struggled with the pain. His strength was gradually fading. Dimba and the others were worried as they watched Omem's condition getting worse.

Dimba thought of reaching Kanem, but the curfew was still on. Instead, he encouraged Omem to endure the pain. The group discussed what to do. They decided to take Omem to a local herbalist for treatment. Cautiously, they brought Omem to the herbalist in the village. He swung into action as soon as he saw the problem. Tani went and informed Omem's parents. When they came, his mother cried bitterly over her son's condition and insisted that he must be rushed to the clinic. However, her husband, knowing the repercussions, refused her suggestion. As an ex-service-man, Omem's father was able to extract the bullet from the leg and control the bleeding, paving the way for further treatment.

CHAPTER 18

At 7am, Nachau became restless on his bed, wondering why Kiringa was attacked despite the tight security and the curfew imposed. He also pondered where the attackers got the guns they used. After the curfew, Nachau rushed to see the commander in charge of security.

When he got to the commander's tent, two guards at the door asked why he had come. Eventually, they allowed him to see the commander. Luckily, the commander, whose name was Kidiki, was attentive when Nachau introduced himself.

"Have a seat," the commander, said.

"Thank you, sir."

"What can I do for you?" Kidiki asked with authority.

"Something makes me restless. I am here to discuss it with you."

"Go straight to the point. I have no time."

"I wonder how Kiringa was attacked despite the tight security."

Kidiki listened uneasily.

"For some days now, some of your boys have been extorting money from people instead of performing their duty. I am sure you know that this action can breach the security arrangements. You need to encourage your boys to do their job faithfully," Nachau explained.

"You mean we are corrupt, that is why the attack happened?" Kidiki asked angrily.

"Your tank is leaking. You need to seal it up before all the water is wasted."

"Sergeant Surgi!" Kidiki shouted.

"Yes, sir," Surgi answered, as he rushed into the tent.

"I give you three minutes to send this man out of my tent!"

"Yes sir!" Surgi responded. "Sir, you have been ordered to leave."

Nachau stood up gently. "I came here in peace, but you rejected me. A crisis is like a disturbed beehive, the bees fly around stinging any person in their way."

"Get out!" Surgi commanded.

"Idiot! No one will teach me how to do my job!" Kidiki said.

"Surgi," Nachau called, as he was going out. "A tree can grow taller than the walls that surround it. Be an instrument of positive change."

Surgi was quiet.

When Surgi returned, Kidiki warned him not to allow Nachau to visit him again. He also ordered him to monitor Nachau's movements.

When Nachau got to their compound, he met Kanem, and Calvin resting on a mat under a tree. Sitting on the mat, Nachau told his colleagues what happened in his meeting with the security commander. He also suggested to his colleagues that they needed to come up with solutions to the crises. Calvin and Kanem agreed.

Before discussing the crises further, Nachau called his wife and told her of the developments. The children all spoke with him. Nachau was happy to know that all his family members were doing well.

Kanem also talked to his wife and children before the meeting. The children insisted that he return as soon as possible because they had missed him a lot. Kanem asked them to be patient, but in spite of his appeal for patience, the children still yearned for his presence at home. Eventually, Nina helped her husband convince the children about the need for his absence.

"The darkest moments for the people of Romen, Kiringa and all of us are ahead. This meeting is important to help us prepare before they come," Nachau stated as they commenced their discussions.

Calvin and Kanem nodded in agreement.

"Crisis resolution experts have identified four stages of crisis. The first is the 'Latent stage,' which means the entry of a problem into a person's life or community. At this stage, it is mostly unseen. Like a pregnant woman, who is unaware of being pregnant at the first stage of conception."

Calvin and Kanem listened.

"The second stage is the 'Escalation.' The crisis that has been conceived begins to grow. A careful mind will see it manifesting itself in different ways."

Calvin and Kanem paid more attention to the explanations.

"The third is the 'Crisis stage.' That is when, like a woman in labour, the crisis is born. Lives and possessions are lost as a result."

"So, we are now in the 'Crisis stage?'" Calvin asked.

"Yes," Nachau replied. "Every crisis is a symptom. Only careful investigations can expose the real cause because there is always someone who is benefiting from every crisis. Unless the root cause is traced, the crisis will often have new faces."

Kanem and Calvin listened.

"There are two aspects in a crisis. One is negative and the other is positive. The negative deals with the present, where lives and possessions are lost, while the positive is in the future, when we learn helpful lessons from past events. Injured today is the police of the future."

Kanem and Calvin listened attentively.

"Problems force the doors of progress to open. Peace on earth is not permanent. It refreshes itself from time to time. Underneath every renovation lies old paint. Balloons cannot resist flying when they are in contact with the wind," Nachau clarified.

Kanem and Calvin still listened with growing interest.

"The fourth stage is the 'Post Crisis.' This is a time when the two sides are forced by their frustrations to negotiate effectively with each other in an attempt to resolve the problem. The right agreements are often reached at this stage, because people listen better when they have suffered from a situation. Frustration oils choices."

Calvin nodded in understanding.

"Many youth who were useful in the crises will react against the new system using the same weapons with which they had been earlier equipped. A frustrated mind is more deadly than the most sophisticated gun. A man who kills another man will never be the same again."

"What can we do now, sir?" Kanem asked eagerly.

"We need more courage to do what is right against evil. I will focus more on the Village Head of Romen so that he can understand the message of love. Once he does that, his new point of view can lead him to a discussion with the Village Head of Kiringa."

"I will not give up until Dimba understands the value of using his potential for God's glory," Kanem said.

"I will focus on Dimba's friends and visit the people of Kiringa with the message of God's love," Calvin stated.

"Will that not be risky for you considering the unsafe situation?" Kanem asked.

"I am sure God will not let me down," Calvin answered.

"Low walls don't prevent tall people from looking into the compound. Let's help the people feel and hear about God's love so that they can value one another," Nachau explained.

 Kanem and Calvin listened.

"We must commit our plans to God in prayer; but before that, let's remind ourselves of one basic fact for introducing change. We should anticipate some challenges and set our minds toward managing them well. Time quenches a fire disaster more than water, but water saves valuable things in the process. We must use the right message and time wisely," Nachau clarified.

Kanem and Calvin were encouraged by Nachau. They held hands and prayed for God's intervention.

CHAPTER 19

The Village Head of Romen fell ill. He invited Kanem to the palace to treat him. Nachau was with Kanem and Calvin when a messenger brought the invitation. They went to the palace together.

On getting to the palace, they were led to the Village Head's room by a palace guard. Lying on a bed, he welcomed them. After an examination, he was diagnosed with high blood pressure. Kanem gave him some drugs and advised him to have sufficient rest.

"How can I rest when all is not well?" the Village Head said.

"Rest is a choice. It is easier to rest, despite the crises, when you know that one day they will end, because you are doing something positive to solve the problem. A restless mind leads to restless health," Kanem explained.

"I need your help. I don't know what I can do to solve the problem," the Village Head responded.

Kanem turned to Nachau and Calvin as an indication for them to speak.

"How strong is the sense of unity between your village and Kiringa?" Nachau asked, having been silent for a moment.

"Politically, we have made major contributions to the development of our Local Government Area," the Village Head disclosed calmly.

Nachau kept quiet as he thought deeply.

"Why did you ask?" the Village Head inquired curiously.

"That means that destroying the unity between the two villages benefits those who have evil political intentions," Nachau remarked.

"There is sense in the direction you are heading," the Village Head stated thoughtfully.

"There is great strength in unity. That is why God brought us together," Nachau stated.

"Someone may be scheming to divide us so that we can lose our strength," the Village Head reasoned.

"It is a possibility," Nachau commented.

The Village Head was in deep reflection.

Kanem and Calvin listened with interest.

"Who do you think is the most frustrated person in this village?" Nachau asked.

The Village Head thought over the question.

Nachau, Calvin and Kanem waited in expectation. Kanem was pondering Nachau's reasoning.

"An old man named Ntedu," the Village Head finally disclosed.

"Dimba's father?" Nachau quickly asked.

"Yes," the Village Head answered. "But why did you ask?"

"The Devil easily gets a frustrated person," Nachau remarked.

The Village Head listened well.

A frustrated person is desperate. He looks restlessly for solutions to his problems. Such a person can be used negatively by anybody," Nachau clarified.

"You are right; but I doubt if Ntedu can be used for such a thing. He is physically challenged and loyal to me," the Village Head remarked.

"I am not accusing him. It is just that in crisis management, you must ensure that your search misses nothing. A proverb states, 'When a horse goes missing, one may dig up anthills in search of it,'" Nachau said.

Calvin and Kanem smiled.

"But the crises were due to the fire disaster," the Village Head commented.

"The fire disaster could be an excuse for other reasons," Nachau stated.

"If this is true, then people must be wicked. How can someone measure success by bloodshed?" the Village Head reasoned.

"Success is often a master. It enslaves those who seek it by any means. It denies them the privilege of sound reasoning," Nachau explained.

Kanem and Calvin listened to the discussions attentively.

"God wants us to love one another no matter what happens. You can end the crises with forgiveness," Nachau encouraged.

The Village Head was quiet for some time. "It will be difficult for me to forgive."

"There is always a bright future in forgiveness. Any forgiveness from you as the head of the village will flow like a stream down to your people. Forgiveness releases both the offended and offender from prison," Nachau emphasized.

"Kiringa people do not deserve forgiveness. What they deserve is vengeance!" the Village Head reacted angrily.

"To end a war, you must learn to give your opponents what they don't deserve. God gave us salvation by grace through Jesus Christ," Nachau said."

"If God is real, why does He allow evil in the world?" the Village Head asked worriedly.

"The focus should be on why we choose to use evil instead of good."

The Village Head listened.

"God has set a standard for how we are to live. The first human beings missed the mark. They lost fellowship with God and as a result were punished by Him. Since then, they have had access to the knowledge of good and evil. They were free to choose from either and be responsible for their actions. Choosing evil leads to death, but good leads to life everlasting," Nachau explained.

Kanem and Calvin started praying silently in their hearts that the Village Head would use the opportunity for being reconciled to God.

"But He was not supposed to allow my little girl to die! My other daughter was raped because of the evil of the Kiringa people. They deserve His judgment!" the Village Head said in tears.

"Those who don't deserve forgiveness also need it. I don't know why all these things happened to your family; but I am sure some day everything will be made clear."

"I feel something moving in my heart in a way that I have never felt before. The way you explain God has brought some light to my state of confusion," the Village Head remarked.

"God is willing to help you see the best part of light if only you will welcome the gift of salvation in Jesus Christ."

"How can I do that? I need rest for my soul. I have tried many options, but I am yet to find relief."

"Simply accept Jesus as your Lord and Saviour," Nachau replied.

"If Jesus can help me, I am willing to let Him to."

"He is not only a Helper, but the Saviour and Lord. He will give you peace that no one can take away from you. We were all restless before we made decisions in the past to serve Him," Nachau explained, as he pointed his hand towards his friends. "You will not regret it if you also decide today."

After a long pause, the Village Head took a deep breath and told Nachau of his decision to accept Jesus as Lord and Saviour. They prayed with him and he welcomed Jesus into his heart.

After the prayer, the Village Head felt happy. "I am feeling calmness in my spirit. The world is looking different," he gently said.

"It is the beginning of fellowship with Jesus. Congratulations!" Nachau stated.

Finally, having returned to their compound, they prayed and thanked God for His faithfulness.

⌃

Nachau's cell phone rang six times before he picked it, because he was praying. He did not want to allow anything to disrupt his prayer.

"Hello, Mr. Lah."

"Good morning, sir."

"Good morning, too. I was praying, that is why I delayed in responding."

"Sorry for disturbing you."

"It is okay. How is your family?"

"My family is fine. How is the situation where you are? I heard of the problems in the two villages."

"The situation is challenging, but God is helping us."

"I suggest you return home since the situation is risky for you and others. We still need people like you to keep this nation on the right track."

"God sent us here beforehand to contribute towards the peaceful development of the two villages. We are here on a mission and there is no turning back. The grace of God is sufficient."

"That is okay. I will send some relief materials to you to help those that have been affected by the crises," Lah said thoughtfully.

"That is very good of you. People are going through tough times here, but I am sure very soon they will experience some relief."

"I hope my contribution will aid to reduce the effects of some problems?"

"It will certainly go a long way," Nachau replied.

"Considering your present situation, would you have time to discuss my case today?"

"Which problem do you want us to talk about? The best advice sometimes comes up in desperate situations."

"Thank you for your concern. My next problem is how to groom effective leaders in my organization. I am worried about the future, because I do not know what will happen when I am no longer alive."

"I am happy you are worried about the future. People that think of how life will be after they have gone often prepare for a better tomorrow. How have you been developing leaders?" Nachau remarked after a moment of silence.

"We often search for and employ leaders from other organizations with the commitment of paying them more. Another way we get leaders is to identify those with leadership potential in our company, send them to school for better training and make them leaders of our various departments."

"These are good ways of developing leaders; but I will share some ways that are also helpful. You should know that everybody is a leader. A person must first lead himself well, before he can lead others effectively.

For instance, if a person leads himself to careless living, you can be sure that he can also lead others on a negative path."

"Self-leadership is a new perspective to me."

"First identify those that are leading themselves well."

Lah listened calmly.

"The principle for today is Banana leadership style is the best."

"What does that mean?" Lah asked curiously.

"Banana trees do not grow alone. They grow in a colony with the young ones. When they grow and bear fruit, they are cut off to enable the younger ones to also grow and bear fruit."

"Sir, you are amazing me with your insight."

"All for the glory of God."

"No one should grow alone," Lah reflected. "That is a good point," he said.

"I am glad you understood the point. I also would like to share the 'GG Principles' of leadership with you."

"What is that?"

"I developed it by God's grace through an assessment I carried out on a particular tribe in our nation. The 'GG' stands for Generation to Generation. The people in the tribe have succeeded in providing and sustaining generations of business leaders."

"How do they do that?"

"Based on what I have learnt, I discovered the following: In line with their main business practice, none of them does business alone. They don't rush into business without training under a mentor. They spend some years learning before they develop business muscles to start their own."

Lah picked a pen and a jotter and started writing.

"As they serve under their mentors, they all have opportunities of practical leadership. If there are three young people under a mentor, one of them is the leader of the two. Once he graduates to start his business, the second is promoted to first position, while the third becomes the second and a new person is brought in to be the third. Continuously, the chain is sustained."

Lah wrote the points quickly.

"They often develop a consistent saving relationship with a specific bank in order to be qualified for a loan to expand their businesses."

Lah continued writing.

"After service, the mentors of the young ones don't send them away empty-handed. They settle them with funds to help them start their businesses. They are free to diversify into other areas of business. They are not restricted to the ones they have learnt."

Lah wrote more points.

"They also utilize the concept of investing their money first and then use the profit later."

"You have really taken time to learn from them. I am able to figure out which tribe it is."

Nachau smiled. "Don't just use the act of saving money; transfer the value to the next generation of leaders. Only available money can be spent."

"How can I be sure that they would use the value after learning it?" Lah asked.

"Be hopeful always. You also need to know that they would certainly make some mistakes. Allow them to be part of developing solutions to their problems. In that way, they would own the values and become channels of transfer to those they lead."

"Thank you, once again, sir. I am really satisfied with your input. I will call again another time. Expect the relief materials for the people soon. Share them at will."

"I will be expecting them. Remain blessed."

CHAPTER 20

Kanem was treating people in the clinic and sharing the love of God with them when suddenly, he saw Dimba and Tani passing by. He excused himself and rushed after them, calling their names.

Dimba and Tani hardly slowed down, but Kanem's persistence eventually yielded a positive result.

"Good afternoon," Kanem greeted them politely.

Dimba and Tani kept quiet.

Kanem saw a wound on Dimba's forehead. "What happened to your forehead?"

Dimba was quiet.

Kanem waited for him to speak.

"I had a cut recently," Dimba answered reluctantly.

"How?"

"I can't tell you."

"Why?"

"It is not your problem! If you don't have anything reasonable to say, kindly allow us to go!" Dimba reacted.

"Come over to the clinic, and let me take care of the wound."

"You don't have to bother. The wound will take care of itself," Dimba remarked.

"Dimba, we need to go quickly," Tani interrupted.

"Give me only five minutes to speak with you," Kanem requested.

"Sorry, we don't have five minutes to spare," Dimba said.

Kanem suddenly felt led to look up at a nearby big tree behind Dimba and Tani. He spotted a man in the tree getting ready with a bow and arrow to shoot at Dimba. Dimba was unaware of the danger. Kanem rushed to Dimba and Tani and pushed them to the ground. Unfortunately, the arrow hit Kanem in his right hand and blood started gushing out.

There was confusion after the shooting. Dimba and Tani, realizing what had happened, ran after the man, who came down from the tree, threw away his weapon and fled. They finally caught him and beat him mercilessly before the security agents came to his rescue. All of them were arrested for interrogation.

Nachau, Calvin and well-wishers came to help Kanem and removed the arrow. On hearing of the attack, the Village Head rushed to Calvin's compound to see Kanem. On arrival, he examined the wound closely and was glad, because the arrow used was not poisonous.

Kanem treated himself. His action in saving Dimba's life was appreciated by the Romen people.

After some hours of questioning, Dimba and Tani were released. The man who shot Kanem was called Muno. He had lost his mother during the last crisis between Romen and Kiringa. He believed that vengeance on the Romen youth was the only way to heal his pain.

Dimba and Tani were restless when they got to Calvin's house to see Kanem. They found him resting on a mat under a tree. Dimba and Tani sat beside him on the ground refusing to sit on the wooden stools that were brought to them.

Nachau and Calvin were also there. After welcoming Dimba and Tani, Nachau and Calvin went out for a walk, because they knew that the time had come for Kanem, Dimba and Tani to understand one another better.

"You are welcome, Dimba and Tani," Kanem said calmly.

"Thank you, sir," Dimba responded, after a short silence.

"I am happy to have you here."

Dimba and Tani did not say a word.

"I learnt that the law enforcement agents have no case against you."

"They have no case against us; but that does not mean we are not guilty. What you did for us today has really challenged us. We have never seen or heard of such a sacrifice. You risked your life to save ours. We are here to thank you for your kindness," Dimba said.

"Let us all thank God for the sacrifice of His Son," Kanem replied.

Dimba and Tani listened curiously.

"Jesus gave His life to save all of us."

Dimba and Tani still listened.

"I know that both of you have been disappointed by the people you trusted; that is why you live the way you do. I assure you that God created all of us for His purpose, which is to give Him glory. It is never too late to make it right," Kanem stated. "For the fact that we are still alive is a proof that we are still useful to God in this world. If you confess your sins to Jesus, and ask Him to come into your lives as Lord and Saviour, you will be saved from the penalty of sin, which is eternal death, to life everlasting," he clarified.

"We really appreciate your encouragement. I am sure we would not have been like this if you had been here earlier. We don't like the way we live. However, we were all forced by our greedy leaders to live this way. We need you to help us become better and more useful to ourselves and other people. Since you can risk your life to save ours, we are sure you love us more than our people do," Dimba remarked.

"When you remember and respond with vengeance to errors of the past, there is no way you can correct the errors of today and tomorrow. Love for your enemies in whatever situation stabilizes you effectively for progress," Kanem explained.

"Would the God you people talk about forgive us despite the evil we have committed?" Tani asked anxiously.

"God is more willing to forgive you than you are willing to ask for it. He sent Jesus His Son to die on the cross for our sins so that whoever believes in Him will have eternal life."

"I want to have a change of lifestyle," Tani stated.

"Me, too," Dimba said, with tears in his eyes.

"Accept Jesus Christ as your Lord and Saviour," Kanem urged with joy.

Suddenly, many people outside the compound started shouting. The confusion was intense. Kiringa people had attacked and killed four Romen people. Dimba and Tani stood up quickly and rushed out to see what was happening. Kanem tried to prevail on them to stay in the compound, but they refused.

Kanem also got up and went out to see for himself what was happening. A crowd had gathered shouting and discussing in anger. He noticed that the security agents had been trying to control the situation, but the people were reluctant to listen to their orders.

Dimba and Tani joined the youth as they mobilized themselves. The crowd moved to the palace of the Village Head.

The Village Head was earlier informed of the situation. Together with his elders, he had been discussing some issues in a meeting. The elders wanted a vengeance mission on the Kiringa people.

When the crowd came to the palace, they stood outside shouting for vengeance despite the presence of the security agents. Dimba and his friends were waiting for orders from the Village Head to attack Kiringa. They knew him as a man who did not accept intimidation.

The elders escorted the Village Head when he came out. He was shocked to see many Romen people asking for vengeance and the large number of security agents. He stood quietly in amazement.

"We want vengeance!" the crowd shouted repeatedly in anger.

The Village Head prayed silently for awhile for God's wisdom in handling the situation. "Ladies and gentlemen," he began, after the prayer. "Beloved Romen people."

The people calmed down to listen to his speech.

"The Kiringa people and us have injured ourselves recently. We have all experienced tears of terror. You all know what happened to my daughters and my compound. I am one of those hurt the most in this village. Whatever happened to me and all of you are all directly my problems," the Village Head said.

The people listened anxiously.

"I used to think that vengeance was the answer to all these problems; but recently, I discovered that it only compounds our problems. We must end these killings through forgiveness and dialogue," the Village Head stated.

The crowd looked at him in amazement, because they had expected that he would provoke them into action.

"It was hard for me to make that decision; but I believe it is the best for all of us. I encourage you to go home. My elders and I will discuss further on the situation," the Village Head stressed.

The people and majority of the elders were not satisfied with the Village Head's position. They stood in disappointment, murmuring against him.

"Please, my people, I assure you that I know what I am doing. Everything will be okay by the grace of God," the Village Head assured them.

Reluctantly, one after the other and in groups, the people went back to their homes grumbling. Dimba and his friends were the most displeased among the people. As young men, they felt it a duty to defend their village from attack. They gradually mobilized themselves for action.

Meanwhile, at the palace, the issue of forgiveness was being tackled with all seriousness. Some of the elders, led by Nupam, who were against it, insisted that the Kiringa people should face the wrath of the Romen people. The Village Head maintained his position for forgiveness.

"What has come over you, your highness? I have never seen or heard you talk like this!" Nupam inquired.

"All these killings will not solve our problems. The Kiringa people are also our people. We have lived in peace with them for many years. What we are experiencing now is a challenge to our friendship. Love must be the leader in this situation. I have made up my mind to end these crises," the Village Head explained.

"Your highness, please tell me what has happened to you that changed you overnight," Nupam insisted.

The Village Head paused for a moment. "I have accepted Jesus as my Lord and Saviour."

Suddenly, there was silence for a short time.

"You mean you have accepted the God of Calvin and the strangers?" Nupam asked in disbelief.

"He is not only the God of Calvin and the strangers, but also our God. I have never experienced the peace I now have. I also want you to experience it and you will understand better what I am telling you," the Village Head stated.

"Your highness, please reconsider your position. Your new belief will not help us," Nupam advised.

"There is no way you can know that if you don't try it. We need to have peace with God before we can have peace with others."

The elders did not utter another word. They only gazed at the Village Head in amazement.

"I am sure that peace will be restored in both villages. God will surely help us out of the terrible situations we are facing."

The elders kept quiet. While none of them challenged the Village Head again most of them were still murmuring against him.

^

Dimba and his friends were in their hide-out discussing their next move.

"Someone has said that 'No-one has a monopoly on violence.' The attack we will launch will be the mother of all attacks. We will destroy everything in Kiringa: male, female, children, animals and buildings. Massacre is the mission!" Dimba announced angrily.

"That will be the mission!" most of the group members shouted.

Ganduro was quiet, thinking about his wife, who might be a possible victim.

"When do we carry out the attack?" Tani asked.

"The day after tomorrow, early in the morning," Dimba replied.

"I advise that we exclude women and children from the attack," Ganduro suggested.

"Why?"Dimba asked quickly.

"My wife is in Kiringa. I don't want to lose her," Ganduro said in concern.

"She ceased to be your wife the day she left your house and our village. It is better you forget about her!" Dimba responded.

"I still love my wife. No matter what happened between us, she is still my wife," Ganduro stressed.

"Only a coward thinks the way you do," Tani said.

"If you call me a coward again, I will show you that I am not!" Ganduro reacted angrily.

"You can do nothing to me. It is an act of cowardice to bring the issue of a woman into the camp of men. We are discussing an important matter, but you are only worried over a woman who may have been in love with another man in Kiringa!" Tani stated harshly.

Ganduro slapped Tani in anger.

Tani in turn slapped Ganduro. The two friends fought each other violently. Dimba and some of the young men had to intervene to stop the fight.

"We can never achieve our mission if we are not united. We are here to plan how to fight our enemies, not our friends. Since Ganduro is worried over his wife, we will be careful when we attack. Her father's house will be spared," Dimba explained.

"Thank you, Dimba, for your consideration," Ganduro said, after a moment of silence.

Dimba was quiet.

Tani did not utter another word. He only gazed angrily at Ganduro.

"We are happy to have one of our warriors back," Dimba announced. "Omem, you are welcome."

Omem lifted up his hand and shouted. "A lion is hard to kill. Nothing stops a warrior from achieving his goal!" he boasted.

"We are warriors, we cannot be stopped," Dimba charged the group.

CHAPTER 21

Nachau, Calvin, Kanem, and Namo sat on chairs in front of Calvin's compound, discussing the tension in the villages. They sensed that Dimba and his friends were up to something bad.

Suddenly, Kanem saw Dimba going home. He rushed after him and asked to speak to him. Dimba responded politely, considering the sacrifice Kanem had made for them.

"How is life with you?" Kanem asked.

"I am doing fine."

"We did not finish our last discussion."

Dimba stared at Kanem.

"Dimba, the day I heard of you and eventually set my eyes on you, I became convinced that with the right encouragement, you can achieve success. Do not allow an unfulfilled dream to frustrate you. There is still hope. I assure you that without Jesus in your life, you cannot experience true success. That is why it is important for you to believe in Him."

Dimba listened calmly.

"Don't misuse your potential. This is your time to make it right with God."

"Thank you, sir, for the love you have shown me. I have one mission to execute. After that, I assure you I will serve Jesus," Dimba said.

"The last time we had a discussion, both you and Tani wanted to respond to God's love, but that was interrupted. Why change your mind now?"

"It is not a change of mind. It is an extension of intention. I promise you that everything will be okay after this mission."

"May I know what the mission is all about?"

"It is a secret, sir."

Kanem was quiet for a moment looking at Dimba in concern. "I want to remind you that there is no time to waste. You are not in control of your life. You don't know when and how it will end. The best moment to do right is now."

Dimba listened thoughtfully.

"The sun rises in the morning and sets in the evening. In between are opportunities for us to live well. Forgive those who have hurt you now. Achieve your potential now. Live in peace with people now. The sunset is coming fast, when you cannot work."

"I assure you that all is well. I know what I am doing."

"I hope so, my friend. I hope the mission you talked about is not vengeance against the Kiringa people?"

Dimba stared at Kanem in silence.

"The Kiringa people are your brothers and sisters. No matter what happens, both of you still have a future together. Today is the best moment you have to be a solution, not a problem."

"Thank you once again for your concern. I will now be on my way home. My father is expecting me."

"Thank you, too, for your time."

Dimba moved away slowly. Kanem stood looking at him. He prayed silently that God would fill the hearts of Dimba and his friends with His love. Suddenly, tears of compassion filled Kanem's eyes as he watched Dimba walking away from him.

^

Dimba and his friends were battle-ready, early in the morning, of the day they had set for the attack. They first smoked marijuana and swallowed hard drugs.

The Kiringa youth were in their houses, because the security agents did not allow them to stay out. The security agents were fifteen in number, all wearing bulletproof vests. They were also ready for combat in view of the intelligence report they had received concerning the Romen youth's plans.

Dimba and his friends reached Kiringa undetected by the security agents. Immediately, they launched random attacks, shooting at many people, buildings and the security agents. The combat-ready squad also fired back. The Kiringa youth came out fighting bravely with bows and arrows. The old people, mostly hunters, used their local guns to defend themselves.

Suddenly, a reinforcement of the security agents arrived and attacked Dimba and his friends. The battle lasted for over an hour. Many Kiringa people, including women and children, were killed. Dimba and many of his gang members were shot. Kunteri was also not spared. Corpses were lying on the ground. Tani lost his life on the spot, but Ganduro and some others escaped. Dimba and Kunteri lay on the ground, struggling in pain and bleeding, when the security agents picked them and took them to the local clinic for medical attention.

The clinic lacked a medical doctor who could take care of the situation properly. The news of the situation reached Romen. The Village Head and others received it with horror. Many people, especially women, wept over the death of their children.

When Kanem was informed of the need for a medical doctor, he did not waste time. He went to Kiringa with Nachau, Calvin and Namo, under tight security escort.

On reaching the clinic, they were shocked at seeing the heavy casualties. The beds were insufficient as a result. Some patients were on the floor. The sight of Dimba lying in a pool of blood on the floor drew the attention of Kanem. Kunteri was lying next to Dimba, but his case was not as serious as that of Dimba. After medical examinations, Kanem knew that Dimba might not survive, for he had lost much blood.

"Dimba," Kanem called.

Dimba, in agony, tried to speak.

"Dimba, please listen to me!" Kanem pleaded in concern, as he made efforts to help Dimba.

The nurses were also busy taking care of other patients. Nachau, Calvin and Namo were involved in rendering help. They also engaged in prayers for the wounded.

"It is still not too late for you to make it right with God. All you need to do is invite Jesus into your heart. He is right now waiting for you to do that," Kanem anxiously encouraged Dimba.

Dimba tried to talk, but his speech was faint. Kanem bent towards Dimba's mouth to listen. "Are you sure Jesus would forgive me?" Dimba asked faintly with tears in his eyes.

"Yes, my friend," Kanem quickly replied.

Dimba appeared relieved by this assurance.

Kanem was very hopeful as he fought hard to help Dimba.

"I want to accept Jesus as my Lord and Saviour," Dimba finally announced.

"Say this prayer after me. Lord Jesus," Kanem hurriedly told him.

"Lord Jesus," Dimba echoed in hope.

"Forgive my sins, and come into my life as my Lord and Saviour."

One word at a time, Dimba repeated the prayer after Kanem. Finally, after the prayer, Dimba felt great calmness in his heart. "Please, tell my uncle, Eremale, that I am sorry," Dimba whispered painfully, after silence for a moment. "We were the ones that hurt him. Tell the Kiringa people to forgive us for all the destruction we brought on them. Tell our Village Head that he was right; love and forgiveness are the best ways to end crises."

Kanem listened anxiously.

"Tell my father, that Jesus is the answer to his problems. Tell our youth, that they should not give up using their talents no matter what happens. Inform them that they can use our natural resources to develop our people. They must only depend on God to succeed, not man," Dimba said faintly, with much struggle, as he breathed his last.

"Dimba!" Kanem called in sorrow.

Dimba was not responding.

Kanem checked his pulse, but there was no hope. Kanem could not control his tears. He stood beside Dimba's corpse pondering the situation. Nachau, who was also in agony, had overheard their discussions. He came to Kanem and comforted him. "The good news is that he has accepted Jesus as his Lord and Saviour. We will see him again someday."

Kanem nodded, but was still in tears.

"His last messages are seeds that will grow one day in Romen and beyond," Nachau said.

Eventually, Kanem was able to overcome his tears. He covered the corpse of Dimba with a bed sheet, and proceeded to tend to other patients, including Kunteri.

Amsami, Malena and Yalami survived the disaster. Their house was not attacked. They quickly came to help Kunteri. When Yalami saw Tani's corpse and heard of Dimba's death, she became worried about her husband's safety. She went round the corpses deposited on the ground outside the clinic, but did not see her husband. She thought probably he did not follow them on the mission or he had been killed and his body left somewhere yet to be discovered. Yalami could not control her tears. She wept bitterly over the situation. Her love for her husband came much more alive than before.

Nachau and Calvin removed their gloves and went out to wash their hands. Calvin spent some time to encourage Kiringa people and to share God's love with them. Some were really encouraged by his message of hope; but many did not pay attention to him because of their sorrow.

Suddenly, Nachau saw Renga, the security agent they had met earlier on their way coming to Romen. This time he was not in uniform. Nachau had earlier discussed with him the equal treatment of people and the evil of accepting bribes. Renga seemed to be in a bad mood.

Out of curiosity, Nachau went to him. "Hello," Nachau greeted.

Renga turned and looked strangely at him without uttering a word.

"I am Nachau Turomale. We met and talked at a security checkpoint some time ago."

"I remember," Renga responded, after being silent for a moment.

"How are you?"

"Not good," Renga replied reluctantly. Suddenly, his eyes filled with tears. He quickly took out a handkerchief and wiped the tears.

Nachau thoughtfully waited for him to calm down.

"I am from this village. My mother and younger brother were killed during the attack. I have just arrived in the village," Renga explained.

"That is hard. I wish you God's comfort."

"I wonder how and where the Romen youth got the kind of ammunition they used," Renga commented, in deep thought. "Somebody must have been sponsoring them," he added.

Nachau was quiet in reflection.

A security agent, who was a friend of Renga, came to him and informed him of the arrest of two people who had supplied weapons to Romen youth. They were arrested on their way to Romen to supply more weapons. One of the security agents they met on duty at the last checkpoint before getting to Romen insisted on checking the van thoroughly. The people offered him a lot of money to let them pass, but he refused to accept it. His colleagues tried to convince him to accept it for them and let the van pass; but he refused to listen to them. His insistence on doing his job eventually yielded a positive result.

Renga, in company with Nachau, went to Romen. On getting there, they saw a blue van surrounded by security agents and many Romen people. The security agents were interrogating the men at their station.

Nachau looked at the van suspiciously and wondered if it was the van he had seen before. The scene of the checkpoint, where they had met Renga came to his mind. Nachau called the attention of Renga to the van. Renga went and looked at the driver closely, because he knew him in view of his frequency in using the road. To his shock, Renga confirmed that the driver was the person he had known. The fact occurred to him that he had been accepting bribes from someone whose business was weapon-smuggling.

Renga moved away from the crowd. He went and sat under a tree crying bitterly. Nachau went to him and sat beside him without saying a word.

"I have contributed to the massacre of my people!" Renga lamented.

Nachau listened.

"The driver I used to accept peanuts from without checking his van was responsible for the arms used against my people," Renga recalled, as he wept bitterly.

"That is why honesty and faithfulness are very important in all we do. Corruption is deadly and its venom spares no one. You have already made the mistake. The lessons from the consequences are what you have to learn," Nachau stated.

"I have been restless since the day you talked to me. Part of the problem is the insistence of some of our senior officers to have a share in the proceeds realized at the checkpoints."

"Everyone can say no to wrong. Your life doesn't depend on what is wrong. You can only have courage in doing what is right."

Renga continued to weep. Eventually, his cell phone rang. He was needed at Kiringa. "I need to go," Renga said, after speaking on the phone, as he moved away wiping his eyes with a handkerchief.

Kidiki, the commander of the security operation, saw Nachau and came to him. He left an officer in charge of the interrogation. Nachau became expectant when he saw him. Several thoughts juggled in his mind.

Kidiki was quiet for a short time when he reached Nachau.

"How are you doing, sir?" Nachau asked.

"I am not doing well. I came to apologize for mistreating you when you came to my tent."

Nachau listened anxiously.

"Your words that day made me restless after you had left. I tried to get over them, but I could not. The death of people here has seriously disturbed my conscience. I feel guilty for not doing my job well. You were right, my tank was leaking."

Nachau listened attentively.

"I have good news for you. We have blocked the leakages. That is why we were able to make good progress. Thank you for your courage, and concern for ensuring that we do our job well," Kidiki emphasized.

"I am happy you realized it at last. I also appreciate you coming to me to share your experiences. This is God's work and we must thank Him for that."

Kidiki stretched out his hand for a handshake. "As from today, I will consider you a good friend," he said, as he shook hands with Nachau.

"Thank you, my friend. I wish you well in your work," Nachau remarked with a smile.

Kidiki smiled back before he left Nachau.

Akio called Nachau a few minutes after Kidiki's departure to know how they were. Nachau told her of the situation. She was sad to receive the bad news of the death of Dimba and others. "Your work among the people was not in vain. No matter what happens, you and your friends have been victorious for God's glory," Akio encouraged.

"Thank you for the encouragement."

"We have been praying for the success of the mission. Be strong and continue to depend on God for the right results. I love you, my dear," Akio emphasized.

"I love you, too. How are the children doing?" Nachau asked.

"They are doing okay."

"Tell them I will see them soon, by God's grace."

"I will tell them."

^

The dead bodies of those killed were given a mass burial by the government to prevent a further crisis. The people in both villages cried bitterly. Suram, Dimba's sister, who had arrived from Mari, wept and rolled on the ground during the period of the burial. The death of her brother was something that would ever linger in her memory. Ntedu too was terribly upset over the loss of his son. He was his hope for the future.

After the burial, the relief materials from Lah arrived as he had promised. The Federal, State and Local Governments also brought relief materials. Despite some diversion of materials by some Government officials, the distribution among the victims of the crises was successful. Nachau, his friends and the Village Head of Romen stood up against any diversion.

The youth who were involved in the crises were arrested and taken to the city for trial. Ganduro, Omem and Kunteri were also among those arrested. Kunteri's condition had slightly improved.

When Yalami heard of the arrests made, she was relieved to know that Ganduro was still alive.

The interrogations of the weapon suppliers resulted in some vital leads. Two wealthy people in the city with huge political ambitions were responsible. This was just as Nachau had earlier imagined. Their motive was to divide the strength in unity between Romen and Kiringa. The insider they used to distribute weapons was also arrested. People were shocked to see that Ntedu was involved, despite his health problems. They wondered what his purpose was.

When arrested and interrogated, Ntedu acknowledged frustration as the reason for his involvement. He had become angry because of the negligence of those who could have helped him. Other reasons he gave for his involvement were to get money to treat himself and support his son, Dimba, to succeed with his plans.

The security agents and leaders of Romen and Kiringa were highly surprised as they listened.

When asked how the people approached him, Ntedu narrated. "I was lying down under a tree in my compound one day. Two men came to my house in a car and entered. They called me by name when they came in. I was surprised when I heard them call my name. On looking more closely, I realized they were my old-time friends. We met in the city a long time ago. They told me of their intention to incite Romen and Kiringa people against each other, to weaken their political strength. They offered me two hundred thousand Naira to work out a plan of action to achieve this."

The security agents and leaders of Romen and Kiringa listened eagerly.

"In addition, they promised me an appointment if they formed a government. I tried to resist their offer, but could not because of my frustration. The fire disaster at the house of the Village Head of Kiringa, after the disagreement over the marital problems between Ganduro and Yalami was a good opportunity for me. The action taken by the

Kiringa people against the compound of the Village Head of Romen was another good platform. I used the phone number the people gave me and informed them of the situation. They promised to supply weapons and someone who would train the Romen youth to fight the Kiringa people."

The security agents and leaders of Romen and Kiringa still listened.

"Eventually, they kept their promise. That was how the Romen youth got the weapons they used against Kiringa," Ntedu narrated in tears. "I have now lost everything. Even my son whom I valued so much is no more. Please, all of you should forgive me!" he pleaded, still in tears.

Some of the leaders became extremely angry and wanted to kill Ntedu, insisting that he did not deserve to live; but the security agents stopped them.

The Village Head of Romen thought deeply on how wicked people could be, just to achieve earthly pleasure that is only temporal. He quickly recalled Nachau's earlier assessment of the crises, in which he asked about the most frustrated person in the village.

The security agents took Ntedu to the city in an open van. On their way out of the village, people, especially women, threw stones at the van and called Ntedu nasty names. Ntedu looked back at the village of his birth. The angry crowd he saw abusing him made him remember how he had been respected before now. He wept bitterly, regretting his actions. The reality hit him hard that based on the magnitude of the offence, he would never return to Romen alive.

CHAPTER 22

The time came for Nachau and Kanem to return home. The Village Head and many Romen people were not happy at their departure. Calvin knew he would miss them very much. Namo came and thanked them for their love and encouragement.

The Village Head of Romen also thanked them for their kindness and efforts among his people. In return, Nachau and Kanem gave God the glory. Kanem had envisioned building a clinic in the village for free medication to aid the suffering people.

The trip back home was interesting. They spent much time discussing what the Lord had done during their stay at Romen. However, Kanem still found it difficult to manage his thoughts about Dimba. Nachau encouraged him again to focus his attention on God's perfect will, believing that the last words of Dimba would not go in vain.

On reaching home, they were welcomed warmly by their families. After two days, the two families and friends came together for a dinner and fellowship at Nachau's house to further thank God for their safe return. Lah and his wife were also among the guests. Nachau and Kanem used the opportunity to share their experiences during the mission work.

As the guests were deep in discussions and refreshing themselves with food and drinks, Nachau invited Lah into his study room. "I noticed that you want a discussion with me," Nachau said, when they entered the study room and sat down.

"Yes, sir," Lah quickly remarked. "How did you know that?"

"Your face betrayed your thoughts."

There was silence for awhile. "I have money and many good things that money can buy; but I am not happy. How can I find peace like you?"

Nachau looked at Lah with joy in his heart.

Lah waited anxiously for a reply.

"Someone said that 'man is restless until he finds his rest in Jesus.' No matter how rich and intelligent a person is, if he is yet to receive Jesus as Lord and Saviour, I assure you that the person is miserable. Jesus has given an open invitation to all those who are tired of carrying heavy loads to come to Him and have rest."

Lah listened keenly.

"The world gives peace that can be taken away from you by circumstances; but Jesus' peace is the type that no one can take away from you. You are more special to God than you can imagine."

"I have done terrible things in life. Would God really forgive me?" Lah asked calmly.

Nachau removed an amount of money from his pocket and pointed it directly at Lah's face. "Let me use this money to demonstrate to you what someone did."

Lah waited in expectation.

"Do you love this money with the new note like this?"

"Yes."

Nachau squeezed it. "Do you still love it as squeezed as it is?"

Lah nodded, indicating yes.

Nachau dropped it on the tiled floor and trampled on it with his shoe. "Do you still love it?"

"Yes," Lah answered, trying to imagine what Nachau was up to.

"'You and I are like the new note. Whether we have been squeezed or trampled by sin, our main value to God remains the same.' God loves us the way we are, more than we can imagine. Jesus died on the cross so that everyone can come, accept Him as Lord and Saviour and be free from the bondage of sin."

Lah was quiet for a short time, thinking. Nachau waited patiently for his response.

"I want to accept Jesus as my Lord and Saviour!" Lah gently said.

"Jesus is willing to come into your heart. Let us pray," Nachau stated gladly.

Both of them held their hands together and prayed.

Nachau smiled after the prayer.

Lah kept quiet for a moment.

"The last principle I will share with you today is the one that you have just experienced. You can do nothing without Jesus."

"Thank you for your encouragement. I pray that God will make me His instrument of blessing."

"He will direct your path. Only depend on Him for guidance."

"I have already started feeling a great burden in my heart towards my family and staff. I will start by improving my relationships with them. They should also discover what I have discovered."

Nachau smiled. "There is no time to waste."

"Thank you once again!"

^

The elders of the two villages had gone through a series of reconciliation meetings. Nachau, Kanem and Calvin had earlier helped them to see the need for these meetings. The Local Government had set up a Committee to investigate the cause of the crises. After a series of investigations, it was discovered that the real cause of the fire disaster was an electrical fault in one of the rooms of the Village Head of Kiringa. The discovery and disclosure of the cause shocked the people and leaders of both villages. Shame and regret overwhelmed the two villages, because many people had lost their lives and possessions due to rumour mongering. Fresh weeping broke out again in both villages. Many people were hugging each other and weeping uncontrollably.

The leaders were also not left behind. Both leaders and people of the two villages gathered at Romen for reconciliation. Nachau and Kanem were invited to attend the meeting. They went together with Lah, Akio and Nina. On arrival, Calvin, Namo, the leaders and people of both villages, warmly welcomed them. Eremale also attended the meeting in a wheel chair, pushed by his wife.

During the meeting, Nachau introduced Lah as one of the supporters of the two villages with relief materials. The heads of the two villages thanked Lah for his support. Many issues were thoroughly discussed during the meeting. Eventually, Nachau and Kanem were asked to speak.

Nachau asked Kanem to speak first. Kanem calmly stood up, and looked at the people with concern and appreciation of the reconciliation process. "I am grateful for the opportunity to contribute to this meeting. Be comforted for all your losses because of the crises. I am happy that today we are correcting our errors and reconciling. I am aware that we have lost many people, especially youth. I was not close to many of them. Dimba was the person I became close to," Kanem said. He paused for awhile, struggling with his thoughts over his relationship with Dimba.

The people stared at him curiously.

"Dimba had a vision of making his life and the lives of others better, but was frustrated by the disappointment he experienced from someone he thought would help him," Kanem explained.

Eremale started crying as he thought about Dimba.

"It is very important for us to help the needy at the time we have the opportunity. Dimba's frustration led him to leading the gang that fought against Kiringa. This would have been avoided if the right person had earlier responded adequately to his vision," Kanem emphasized.

Eremale broke into a loud cry. "I am the one he came to for help. I really regret my action!" he lamented, as he interrupted Kanem's speech.

Many people turned and looked at him. Some of them hissed in dislike because they knew him as a stingy man.

"I suspect that I am in this condition because I refused to help him. There must be a connection between the armed robbers who attacked me and the late Dimba. I felt in my mind that the leader of the gang was Dimba!" Eremale said in tears.

"Don't make false accusations here!" Suram, Dimba's sister, reacted furiously.

Eremale, still in tears, looked at Suram.

"Please, calm down, I have something to say about that," Kanem pleaded.

Eremale and the others were calmed in expectation.

"You were right, Dimba was the leader of the gang who attacked you," Kanem announced.

Most of the people were surprised.

"I knew it!" Eremale stated. "I knew it!" he added, pointing his hand at Suram.

"He confessed it to me when he was dying. He asked me to tell you that you should forgive him," Kanem informed him.

Mem, Eremale's wife, was sad about this development. Her face indicated it clearly. The people were quiet, eagerly waiting for what Eremale would say. Eremale also was quiet for a moment. "There is nothing I can do now against him, he is already dead," Eremale said, still shedding tears.

"I will never forgive him," Mem interrupted angrily. "He made us waste money and pass through serious agonies!"

Most of the people turned towards Mem and looked at her strangely.

"Dimba does not need your forgiveness. You are responsible for your husband's stinginess, which is why he refused to help us. I don't blame my brother for doing what he did. I would have done worse if I had been given the opportunity!" Suram reacted bitterly.

"You have no right to talk to me like that! Don't forget that I am your uncle's wife!" Mem said in anger.

"Enough of all that! We are here to reconcile, not to dig out more reasons for hatred," the Village Head of Romen cautioned.

Mem and Suram became quiet. Eremale continued to sob.

"I am sorry for opening up old wounds. That wasn't my intention. But I needed to give the background to my conclusion. I would like to close my speech by reading to you the last words of Dimba, because I felt they would be helpful in our present situation," Kanem stated, while looking at Nachau and the Village Head of Romen. They both nodded in support of his wish.

"I took the time to write them down because I was sure they could be stored in memory of Dimba," Kanem remarked, as he removed a piece of paper from his pocket.

The people were quiet in expectation.

"Please, tell my uncle, Eremale, that I am sorry. We were the ones that hurt him. Tell the Kiringa people to forgive us for all the destruction we brought on them. Tell our Village Head that he was right; love and forgiveness are the best ways to end crises. Tell my father, that Jesus is the answer to his problems. Tell our youth, that they should not give up using their talents no matter what happens. Inform them that they can use our natural resources to develop our people. They must only depend on God to succeed, not man," Kanem read. "Thank you for listening," he added and sat down.

There was silence. The people were looking at one another. Dimba's message was timely. Eremale continued to cry. Mem also looked worried. The message made her think deeply.

Nachau saw the opportunity as the right time for him to deliver his speech. He stood up slowly and greeted the people with respect, beginning with their leaders. "Ladies and gentlemen; my brothers and sisters. We thank God for using Dimba's confession to unveil some important issues. I want you all to know that whenever there is war, many people lose their lives and possessions; but to some, it is a source of income, power and control. 'People who sell weapons get many customers during war.' Those who engage in fighting eventually develop a culture of violence. Their children will grow up to adopt it as the best way for solving their problems," Nachau explained.

The people listened with keen interest.

"A story is told of a married man and his wife, who had been praying for twenty years, because they were childless. One day, God sent a Child, Money and Patience for them to choose one and have the other two returned to Him," Nachau stated.

The crowd was still attentive, listening patiently.

"There was a big river to be crossed on the way leading to the man's house. Patience, the only one who could swim, helped the Child and

Money to cross. When they got to the house, they knocked at the door. They informed the woman of their mission when she opened the door and saw them. The woman went inside and discussed it with her husband."

The people were still attentive.

"The husband suggested that they choose the Child, but the woman insisted on choosing Money. As a result of the disagreement, the man went out and chose Patience. The Child and Money left the house for a journey back to God. Eventually, they came to the river, but Patience was not there to help them cross. After some time, they decided to return to the family and live with Patience. Finally, the family got all the three because the man chose Patience," Nachau narrated.

Most of the people smiled at Nachau in appreciation of the story.

"Similarly, when you accept Jesus as your Lord and Saviour you will be saved from bondage of sin and have eternal life," Nachau explained.

Many people nodded in understanding.

"There is still hope for you in Jesus even if you consider yourself the worst sinner. We are all special to God and that is why we are still alive so that we can complete the purpose of our lives in this world, which is to glorify Him."

The people still maintained silence, listening more attentively.

"God wants us to live in love and unity. There is no way we can have genuine progress outside love. We must love God and love our neighbours before we can enjoy life. It is only through love that we can easily realize our full potential. Instead, we have killed our brothers and sisters, and have also destroyed many of our possessions."

The crowd broke the silence and wept bitterly over those lost to the crises.

"If we come to God with sincere hearts and seek for His forgiveness, He will forgive us and help us to become better. God is willing to help us enjoy the future more than the present." Nachau continued to speak passionately, helping the people to discover the love of God. His speech sank deep into their hearts. As a result, many of them gave their lives to Jesus. Eremale, Mem and Suram were among the first to do so. Amsami and his wife, Malena, also responded. Malena came to her husband where he was seated and hugged him. Both of them were in tears.

Many people from both villages also hugged each other and cried bitterly, asking one another for forgiveness. Yalami was also part of the conversion experiences. She approached her mother and apologized for what she did to her earlier. Malena also asked for forgiveness from her daughter because of her attitude to her and her husband. They hugged each other in tears.

ᴧ

The new believers were eventually handed over to the Church that Namo was pastoring, for discipleship. Calvin spent some time encouraging believers and training them in evangelism. The Church received great support from Nachau, Kanem and Lah. A new building was built for fellowship. After ensuring that the Church was standing strong, Calvin felt the leading of the Lord to relocate to another village. Namo was very grateful to God for the support they had received.

Eremale made up his mind to make Dimba's vision come alive in memory of him. With his wife and Suram, they founded an organization and named it DREAM OF DIMBA, to facilitate the involvement of youth in exploiting the rich natural resources that abounded in both Romen and Kiringa. Kanem became the leading fundraiser for the organization. Nachau and Lah were also of great help. Many people were assisted to develop themselves and go to school.

Lah also started a huge rice farm in Romen. Several of the Romen and Kiringa people were employed as workers on it. His leadership quality had improved greatly.

Many of the Romen and Kiringa youth became self-employed in both rainy and dry season farming. As a result, they became the major food producers in the state. Many people came from far and near to buy grains and vegetables from them.

Yalami was finally reconciled with her husband. She visited him often in prison until the time he was bailed out by his parents, while the case continued in court. Ganduro also accepted Jesus, and they eventually had a Church wedding. They became a lovely family and hardworking farmers. God blessed their family with a baby girl. They named her Ercaru, which means love.